The Blue

Sarah Carvajal

Sarah Carvajal

*For my mom and dad who always encouraged me to chase
my dreams and persevere*

Chapter 1

The Waking Life Ends

A coolness swallows my limbs, starting from my fingertips and toes until it consumes my entire body. The darkness isn't unwelcoming or scary, but instead quite peaceful. I lift open my eyelids, no longer feeling the same heaviness as before. The light from the moon pierces my gaze before settling into a strange indigo hue over the night sky. Wrapping my arms around myself I rub at the swollen skin around my cracked ribs to find it's no longer cold, bruised, or screaming, but also not its usual creamy white color. A splash of water comes up from the edge of the river, passing right through my pale legs, disappearing into the gravel and sand mixture beneath them. I stare down at my legs, confused. Not only because the water didn't touch my legs but because of the lack of pain or deformity. I run my hand over the almost light-blue-colored skin on my leg, slightly relieved when the pads of my fingertips push against my shins and the familiar feeling of textured skin and pressure register in my brain through my nerves. I swore my left leg snapped in a strange direction when the frozen waters slammed my body into a particu-

1

larly sharp rock. I remember the shooting pain spiking up my shin, followed by the stinging sensation of exposed flesh and nerves to dirty waters as bone shredded through muscle and tissue getting caught on the rock that snapped it in two, red water surrounding me. Flashes from a deep burgundy to neon red bleeding into my vision and a burning sensation in my throat.

I must have passed out from the pain or blood loss. I wince at the memory from just moments ago, confirming that it's real. I'm not crazy.

"Are you looking for something?" A small, polite voice asks, making me jolt upright from my spot on the rocks, my toes digging into the wet gravel. Looking up I see a young girl, no older than six, staring down at me. I stare back at her, confused as to how she got here. I swear no one comes out here late at night; I was there to check the area before, and no one was here.

She clasps her hands behind her back, pushing out her little chest, waiting patiently for my response. I just stare at her, dressed in an old-fashioned pink frilly dress you'd see on your great grandmother's Madame Alexander dolls, confused. I look closer at her, seeing her pale face glowing a light shade of periwinkle. If it wasn't for the sweet look on her face, I'd think she was something out of a horror movie because she appeared so suddenly. I look around at the unfamiliar part of the river, realizing that I'm much farther from the bridge than I thought. I must have drifted down quite a way before resurfacing.

"Oh, you must be new," she states, her blonde ringlets bounce as she shifts her head to the side, her eyes widening for only a moment as if she just put something together that she wasn't expecting.

I stay silent as she walks around, her bare feet crunching against the ground with each step. Her honey-colored eyes graze over the surface of the river as if searching for something, not bothering to tell me what she's doing. She huffs, neither of us saying a word as she trots back over to me, staring into my eyes once more, still searching. I look back into her troubled eyes, no longer thinking she seems as youthful as her body appears. Instead, her eyes express the mind of a grown woman, worn down and yet enlightened in a way that only comes with age. I consider asking, but then think better of it. If she is older than she looks, she might be insecure about it or irritated by my rude questions. I haven't even said anything back to her yet, and she's staring so intently at me. What a strange girl.

Neither of us says a word for a while, the sound of the rushing water and singing insects filling the silence between us, as I let her have a moment to pull her thoughts together.

"Well, it looks like you had a bit of a rough go of it, might need a place to stay for a little while. You can stay with us until you move on," she finally concludes, holding out her hand for me to shake.

I stare at her hand for a second, feeling a bit unsure about her meaning, but decide to take her hand anyway. Her small hand feels warm against my cool skin, still chilled by the water I suppose. She gives me a firm handshake before tightening her grip and gently yanking me up from the ground. The world around me seems to shake, my vision blurring a bit. I must be disoriented from the river's roughness.

"I'm DD by the way. You don't have a name yet, do

3

you," she probes, turning on her heel to walk away from the river, expecting me to follow her to who knows where.

I go to protest and tell her my name, opening my mouth only to find no words come out. I have a name. I just can't seem to remember it. My head spins, trying to think of the name I've been called for the past sixteen years but nothing comes to mind. Distant memories and familiar but unknown faces flash through my head, all their lips forming to shape a name that is my own, like a slow-motion slideshow except no sound or solution comes out. I've got to have a name, so why can't I remember it? Maybe I hit my head against a rock and that's why I passed out. I should get that checked out later, just in case. I'll have to tell the hospital my name though, so how will that work? My name–what's my name?

"Seriously," she says, her voice lowering a bit, her body completely halting to look back at me. "Don't stress about it. It happens to all of us the moment our waking lives end. If you think about it too long, you'll go mad. Then no one can help you."

I stand completely still for a moment, realizing what she said. I'm not going crazy. I did get hurt. I died. I'm dead. But how is this possible? I'm walking. I'm breathing. Wait, am I breathing?

Or maybe I'm crazy already?

"I should've been a little clearer when asking," she starts, leaning up against a grayish boulder that must have been moved there since it doesn't seem to blend in with anything else in the area. "You haven't run into any others yet, have you?" Her tone dips lower once more, almost as if she's testing me.

"Others?" I question.

"Never mind," she sighs, her body relaxing back into its

earlier, more chipper state. She turns back around to continue walking toward wherever she was originally taking me, and we fall into a comfortable silence.

The sound of the rushing river starts to fade as we move up the grassy hill. A small, worn-down tackle shack sits a few yards away from the empty road, the old, white paint skinning itself off the rotting wood siding. I try to make out the chipping red letters on the sign above the door, but all I can put together is a capital "B" and half a "k". Long strands of unkempt grass pass through me as we walk closer to the rectangular building, the stench of rotting carp seeping its way to my nose. For some reason I find myself wanting to scratch at my skin where the strands would have touched, but I hold myself back, feeling as though the itch is irrational. As we get closer to the door, I realize that DD intends to go into the shack, and I wonder how she plans to open the glass door. A sudden wave of hope strikes me that I might be able to feel things again. Maybe DD will be my ticket to learning about this new life as a ghost of sorts. The idea of hope instantly dissipates, turning into shock when I watch her little body move straight through the glass. Words fail me as a cackle sort of laugh echoes from within the tackle shop. I try to follow her through the glass but stop short, not fully convinced that I'll be able to walk through like she did. What if I slam into the door or get caught halfway? Another laugh rips through the air.

"Oh, you've brought a real entertainer this time, DD," a deep voice chokes out between his laughter. "She's like a chicken trying to peck at the door, not realizing that it's just glass."

"Oh, shut it you, dunderhead. She's new and doesn't get how being in the in between works yet," DD scolds, reaching her arm back through the door, pulling me through with more strength than I realized she had. Just like the grass and the gravel from before I felt nothing.

"I can tell she's a freshie, dear DD. That much is obvious," the almost snarky voice says again.

I look away from the door, still in awe, to find a thin, lanky man, probably not much older than me, sitting criss-crossed on the cemented floor. He cocks his head to the side, openly examining me in his old-timey three-piece suit, slowly twisting his gold pinky ring around his finger as if he were some sort of mob boss waiting on a subordinate to fess-up about their wrongdoings. The same thin coating of blue film that seems to envelop both DD and I engulfs his body as well, and I register him as a dead person as well. His thin lips twist into a lopsided smile as our eyes meet, somehow knowing that I figured out what he wanted me to figure out.

"I'm Travis, by the way, as in Lake Travis. You got a name yet, Freshie?" he asks, casually hoisting himself up off the ground, brushing off non-existent dust off his shoulder. Can we even collect dust on our clothes? I look down at my own ribbed tank top and jeans and realize they are completely dry. "What are you freaking out about now, Freshie? Are you sad that you died in uncomfortable pants and have to wear that for all eternity or something?"

"No," I snap, getting tired of his condescending tone. "I'm just wondering how I'm not soaking wet from being in the river, but I guess nothing seems to make sense here."

"The river? What were you doing in the river?" Travis asks, looking back at DD. She just shakes her head. "Ah, I see. I guess we could just call you that then, since DD found you there. Your new name is River." I just nod, not really understanding but still liking the idea of having a name of my own again. River. I could get used to that.

"Since DD brought you here, I guess I don't mind if you

stay at our pad for a while," he says, looking down at me, slinging one of his arms around my shoulders. "Us Wanderers need to stick together. Don't you agree, DD?"

"Don't start with me, Travis," DD snaps back, glaring back at him as if there was a double meaning in what he said. "Don't try to drag River into your shenanigans."

"I'm not dragging anyone anywhere," he replies, lifting his arm back up off my shoulder, walking over toward an irritated DD. "I'm just simply saying that it'd be nice if Wanderers supported each other and had each other's backs."

"What's a Wanderer?" I ask before DD has the chance to respond and this argument heats up anymore.

DD sighs, her eyes softening as she averts her gaze from Travis to face me. "We are the ghosts that stay in the in between. Most people are able to pass on not long after they come to the in between: their bodies put to rest, usually through burial or cremation nowadays. Wanderers, on the other hand, just linger here a bit longer."

"Linger," Travis snorts, rolling his eyes before looking back at me. "What DD means to say is that we are stuck here in this in between sort of realm, because no one found our bodies or cared enough to look. We're forgotten nobodies, who now have to sit and watch the living live like it's some sort of sitcom, but our own lives are on an ever-looping pause. So, congratulations and welcome to the Wanderers' Club!"

An unexplainable tinge of pain tightens around my chest at the revelation. No one cares about me. No one is bothered that I'm dead. I'm just dead. Was my waking life really that horrible? Someone had to care about me. A small pulsing ripples through my head as I try to force myself to remember. I go to massage my temples hoping to relieve some of the tension so I can focus on the blurred woman's face in the back of my mind.

"River, stop!" DD shouts, ripping my hands away from my head, cutting off my train of thought. "The number one rule we have is to forget about your past." she pauses, her eyes almost glassing over making her look even more doll-like. "There is a reason we don't have our memories. You might be tempted to investigate your waking life. You might feel drawn to people or places from the past or have feelings summoned that you can't explain. Ignore them. That's the only rule if you want to stay with us."

The room falls silent. I almost expect Travis to crack a joke to ease the tension, but he doesn't. Instead, he just sits back down on the concrete floor, seeming overly interested in the design on his pinky ring as DD walks back out the front door. I sit on the floor next to him, not sure what else to do. I'm not sure what to think of DD's rules either, or what to think about any of this, really.

Do I wanna stay with them? I guess I don't really have any other option, do I? It's not like I completely understand what's happening or know anyone else around here.

I wonder why she insists we don't investigate our pasts. The only thing I do know is that the look on her face as she said it made it seem scarier than death. It's ironic, comparing something to death now.

"Don't stress about it so much. About what DD said," Travis says, not looking up from his fingers. "Don't ask her about it any further. If you have any questions, you can ask me. Not saying I'll give you all the answers you want though. DD can be a bit of a wet rag sometimes, but she means well. I've known her for a long time. She used to be more fun, then she had to go and grow up on me."

"She does seem a bit serious," I laugh, finding it funny

that he's the one giving me this sort of pep talk since he seemed like such an ass five seconds ago. "I guess I wouldn't mind hanging out with you guys for a bit longer though." I glance over at him and see a thin smile sneak onto his lips for a second before it disappears as he lazily fixes his gaze on me once more.

"Seriously though," he starts, his eyes darkening. "Don't mention anything about our waking lives to DD."

"I won't," I reply quickly, feeling the uneasy tension build up in the room once more. Travis stares me down for a moment as if looking deep in my soul for some sort of understanding, before nodding his head. He closes his eyes and throws his arms behind his head as he lays down, nonchalantly stretching out on the floor.

I spent the next few days alone in the backroom attached to the tackle shop, trying to wrap my head around everything. I'm dead. I have no memories from my past life and, apparently, I can't try to remember, or I won't be able to stay with the only two people I know exist. Well, at least the only other people that are also dead. The first night I overheard DD telling Travis to give me some space, and I'm glad she did. DD was kind and really patient with me, offering a place for me to stay, but I'm not sure what to think of Travis. For some reason, I feel like I can trust them, but I'm still not sure why. Maybe it's all part of my new ghostly instincts or superpowers.

I stare intently at the shortest stack of rusted tin bait containers that I've been trying and failing to move for what feels like hours. It's difficult to tell how much time passes as a Wanderer. We apparently don't need to eat or sleep, since we aren't alive anymore. I try to focus all my energy on my pointer finger, squeezing the rest of my fingers into a fist as if the harder I squeeze and concentrate the more likely my pointer finger will materialize in the real world and connect with the top can of expired salmon. I hold my breath, slowly moving my finger closer to the can, my whole arm shaking with tension. Just as my finger gets close to the beveled edge of the can, it disappears into the metal, like it has one hundred and seventy-eight times already.

"Come on," I whisper-shout, banging my fists on my thighs.

"It's not going to work, no matter how many times you try," DD says from the doorway behind me.

"I'm coming to the same conclusion. I just don't want it to be true," I say, flopping on the floor and letting out a dramatic sigh.

"I'm not going to make you come out if you don't want to, but I wanted to invite you to walk down to the lake with Travis and me. Travis said there is going to be some sort of light show," she says, smiling down at me as she comes further into the room. I close my eyes, not sure if I really want to go or not, wanting to wallow a bit more before just accepting my fate as a dead person. "Apparently there is a lantern festival, and a bunch of people are releasing lights into the night. I thought it sounded really fun, but you don't have to decide right now if you don't want to."

"Thanks, DD," I say, sending her a soft smile, knowing that she's trying to make me feel better.

"We'll be heading out in a few minutes if you want to join us," she says, leaving me to my own devices once more. I hear DD tell Travis that I'm probably not going before their conversation muffles and disappears, the two of them leaving the tackle shack, most likely heading toward the lake.

I roll over on my side, wishing I could sleep. Despite not being hungry, I wish I could eat something. I would do anything for a club sandwich right now. I'm never going to be able to taste food again or do anything as simple as read a book or throw a ball. At least I have DD and Travis to talk to. Maybe there are other Wanderers out there that are as nice as they are.

I suddenly feel bad for not going with them to the lake. Maybe I should follow them. Maybe it'll make me feel better, and I won't feel as stuck as I do now. Maybe they can help me figure out what I'm supposed to do now that I'm dead. I have so many questions about this new reality, and they are my best chance at answering them. I sit up and stand, feeling confident in my decision before running out the door and toward the lake.

My feet seem to know where they are going, my body somehow knowing where the lake is despite my mind not registering it. Blades of grass whip through my shins as I race down the hill. I'm able to make out DD and Travis's shapes as I pass a grouping of trees growing at a slant, slowing down a I get closer to them. DD hesitates by the edge of the lake, whereas Travis dives deep into the endless crowd of people, all clustering in little groups around the rim of the lake. Each group works at a different stage in the lantern building process, some taking time to draw marker flowers or stars, while others write heartfelt letters to their loved ones who have passed on. I notice a group of stupid college age boys drawing dicks on theirs and a small snort escapes my nose. I walk up to DD, following her gaze as she stares out at one lantern that's floating alone on the lake, drifting farther away from the shore. Someone else must have placed their lantern in the lake prematurely; the contrast of the lone lantern making the lake water look much darker than it did before.

Giggling breaks my attention from the singular lantern; a group of teenage girls separate from the crowd, their hands filled with multicolored markers and a folded pre-made paper lantern. I raise my hand to wave at them as they start heading straight toward me, but none of them move to acknowledge me. I quickly jump out of their way as they walk past me, nearly knocking me over.

"Hey," I yell at them, slightly irritated by their rude behavior, but also recognizing that they are just kids. None of them seem bothered enough to turn around and apologize, the three of them plopping down by a large rock to use as a makeshift desk for them to draw on.

"The living can't hear you," DD says, turning toward me.

"Hey," I yell again, waving my arms as I walk closer to the girls trying again to get their attention, not wanting to believe it. Nothing. I reach out my hand to grab one girl's shoulder, not caring how creepy or rude I may seem to them if they were to respond. Instead of meeting the young girl's boney shoulder the momentum of my hand practically melts through her body like cotton candy on a wet tongue.

I snap my hand back, staring and massaging at my wrist as if it were burned or broken but I felt nothing: it was as if I just waived my hand in the air. Part of me wanted to hold out my hand once more to see if my eyes were playing tricks on me, but the thought of my hand moving through someone's body feels vomit inducing.

"You can only interact with other deceased people. See," she says, crouching down and running her hand back and forth in the girl's body, her whole forearm disappearing in the girl's torso as if she were doing something as simple as brewing her morning tea.

Seeming to realize my shock, DD slowly reaches out her hand to touch mine. Her delicate fingers wrap around mine and I all but jump at the contact, half expecting for it not to work. Her small hand feels warm in mine, despite neither of us being alive. Although I had shaken her hand before when we first met, I was a little too focused on processing my own death to realize that we've touched before. It may be trivial but being able to touch her is somewhat comforting.

My first night outside of the tackle shop felt never-ending. You would think not needing sleep would be infinitely refreshing; however, it couldn't be more of the opposite. Staring out into the dark abyss that night after the rest of the waking world went to sleep, the bluish hue that now coated my entire world disappeared and I could almost imagine being alive. DD, Travis, and I were just old friends on a lake trip, taking a break from our real lives out in the ether somewhere. I quickly realized that image was just a dream, when the green sun came up and the indigo hue of my new death took over.

DD and Travis make it easier though, although they are both reluctant to talk about anything regarding our purpose as ghosts or our waking lives. Even though DD and Travis have been nothing but welcoming, I can't help but still feel like an outsider taking up space in their home. The old tackle shack is anything but luxurious, but it's still their home and they've invited me to stay here. The walls are covered in mold and chipped paint, and the smell of rotting fish is probably tattooed into the shack so deep that a facelift would never be able to take away the scent. Despite all that, there is something about this place that feels safe and secure.

I put my hand through a stack of fishing line towards the back of the store, making sure Travis isn't around to make fun of my amazement. Travis, apparently, thinks it's the 'funniest thing in the world' that I get freaked out by the fact that we can't touch anything. Everything here feels unreal though. Sometimes I think it's just a strange dream— no, nightmare— I can't wake up from.

No one alive can see or hear me, not that many people wonder out this far away from town. The tackle shack is pretty much in the middle of nowhere, which is probably why DD chose it. I didn't need to be here long to figure out the DD makes most of the decisions. Despite Travis's matter-of-fact attitude and powerful personality, he seems to fold the moment DD contradicts him or tells him to do something. There's just something about her personality that makes you trust not only her intentions but also her judgment. It's as if she has more life experience than both of us.

"Hey River," DD yells from outside.

I quickly pull my hand away from the fishing line and pop up off the ground before responding, still not wanting to get caught by Travis. "Yeah," I reply, trying to think of something to do with myself so that I look believably busy, as if I were a little kid and she is my parent about scold me and force me to do my chores.

"You wanna go on a little adventure with me?" she asks, sticking just her head through the wall, making her look like a prized deer mount acting as a poor excuse for a man's version of décor. I try not to giggle at the thought before processing what she said. Wait...That means we'd leave the tackle shack!

"Yes!" I all but shout in response, not bothering to ask any questions about what she means by adventure, just elated to do something other than sit here with my thoughts.

"I found this place that's like a junkyard but also art at the same time," she explains, her statement sounding more like a question then a description.

"Sounds interesting," I reply, trying not to flinch as I walk through the wall, but ultimately failing miserably.

"You'll get the hang of it sooner or later," DD says, trying to comfort me. "Being dead isn't an easy thing to get used to." She laughs at her own joke, leading the way to the junk-art-thing she mentioned.

I follow her, awkwardly trying to avoid stepping on muddier looking patches of dirt only to quickly realize I'm being ridiculous; the mud wouldn't stick to my feet even if I wanted it to. DD graciously doesn't comment on my antics, walking silently through the muddy areas with ease. I watch her small feet curiously, stepping along the dirt path, her skin and muscles molding to the shape of the ground and popping back into place with each step. I walk behind her, trying to focus on my own bare feet, pressing into the ground only to realize I can't feel the ground at all. I can imagine the feeling of dirt and mud between my toes as if it was engulfing them now, but I can't make it so. How strange.

I want to ask DD about it, but I know she'll only refuse my questions. Without asking, I've been able to pick up on a few things about this 'world of the dead.' It doesn't seem like any of us age after we've died, which would explain why DD doesn't seem to act like a normal six-year-old. I've also come to realize that there isn't a need to sleep or eat anything since we don't need to grow like a normal living being.

I'm not sure why, but that last part seems to bother me the most. I feel like I'm missing out on the taste of pizza and burritos. Burritos especially. Creamy beans and cheese melted around juicy slices of beef all wrapped in a fluffy tortilla. My mouth is already watering at the thought.

It's strange that I can remember what burritos taste like without having any memories of ever eating one. I couldn't even pick one up and try it if I wanted to. The lack of any memories might be what scares me more than anything about this ghostly existence. It seems that anything of importance, separating me from the rest of the world, is gone. Nothing that could define my sense of self remains, but I am able to remember random, seemingly unimportant things like the taste of beef burritos.

DD says not to think about it too much, but I can't help myself from wanting to know who I am. It's like there is a giant part of myself that is missing, and I have no way to get it back.

"We're here," DD says, taking me away from my thoughts. "Isn't this place just Coolville?"

I raise my gaze from the ground to see a giant pile of deteriorating discarded items tied together with wires and glue towering over us. What on earth is this? DD rushes forward, and I can't help but laugh at her excitement toward what seems like a pile of crap.

"This makes me miss meal-in-a-molds," she says, pointing at a round baking tin with a hole in the center.

"A what?" I question, only able to imagine those tins being used to make pineapple upside-down cake.

"You know, meal-in-a-molds," she says with a shrug, as if I should just know what she's talking about by that simple explanation. "Jello dinners? You know, the giant round jello molds filled with salad and ham rolls or shrimp and peas," she explains further making me visibly gag. "Whatever! You just don't know what you're talking about. Meal-in-a-molds are the best. I'd offer to make you one, but for obvious reasons I can't," she says, waving her arms above her, twiddling her fingers imitating a ghost.

I'm not sure what kind of life she lived before dying, but the thought of eating gelatin and shrimp together makes me want to vomit and die all over again. She just laughs at my reaction, walking around the pile before pointing something else out.

"I wonder what this was used for," she says, looking up at me as if I would know the answer. I shake my head at her antics, walking around the tower to get a better look at whatever she's curious about. I try not to laugh at her again, when I realize she's pointing toward a rusting floppy disk glued to the front of a bicycle wheel.

In moments like I'm reminded that DD comes from a different time. It makes sense that she wouldn't know what a floppy disk is, seeing as she probably wasn't alive when they were created. Apart from her clothes and sometimes her choice of words, DD looks like a little girl but acts like a grandma. It would make sense if she was born around the same time someone the age of a grandmother to me would be. She's just trapped in a little girl's body.

Sometimes though, her excitement feels almost child-like; her personality shifts so quickly and seemingly at random that it almost gives me whiplash. It's like she reverts to being a kid for a second, then it's gone. There is so much about the world of the dead that seems uncontrollable and unexplainable.

"Riv, look! It's a bunch of rubber duckies in a toilet," she giggles, and I can't help but smile at her, skipping from one thing to the next.

"Why would someone do that? It's so silly," I say, examining the duck-filled toilet sitting at the base of the tower.

"It's fascinating, right?" DD says, her voice returning to its usual grandma-like state. "To see what the human mind will come up with and find value in."

"This is a bit bizarre," I say, gesturing to the tower of junk in front of us. "I guess that's art, though. It's usually bizarre and unexpected."

"I'm not sure about other pieces of art, but I like this piece," she says, tilting her head upwards to see the entirety of the piece, emphasizing her small appearance. "I think the concept is fantastic: recycling things that other people have forgotten about, giving them a new meaning. I quite like that concept."

She doesn't look at me, but instead smiles softly at a small blue gnome wrapped in wires that attach it to a mesh wall. I glance back at the floppy disk behind us and suddenly realize why she brought me here. This tower of discarded junk is like us.

"We are just that: discarded junk," I snort, running a hand through my hair. "There is a difference between us: this stuff can all be reused by someone else and reappreciated by the world, whereas we can't have our clocks started again. We're just frozen in time in this in-between realm, forgotten by everyone in the waking world. There isn't any hope for us to be remembered and repurposed."

She doesn't respond or look at me.

We fall into silence, neither of us moving to say anything, and I start to feel bad about my cynical comment. She was just trying to make me feel better and get me out of the tackle shack. Then I ruined it.

Part of me wants to take it back, but we both know it wasn't a lie. Maybe I shouldn't have said anything. I should've just let her show me more of the sculpture, talking back and forth about the multiple uses of each different object, sharing stories about what they could have been or where they could've come from. Maybe she would've gone into a mini-lecture about the hopes for our lives in this in-between realm, talking about all the possibilities and highlights she's had so far. Maybe I would've ended up at the same cynical conclusion, but at least I would've let her think I was a part of the happy delusion that we still have a purpose after our deaths.

I open my mouth to say something but then think better of it, turning to head back to the tackle shack without looking at the rest of the sculpture.

Chapter 2

The Draw

Graffiti murals decorate many of the otherwise empty alleyways, some of which expressing rather beautiful depictions of people who have passed on or fictitious beings of the fantastic. I can't help but let out a small laugh, as I am technically both of those things now. We walk by skyscrapers, seeming much bigger up close than they did back by the tackle shack. The only similarity between the outskirts to downtown are the run-down ma and pa shops. Squished together along each side the road, I wonder if the owners of these places may have started out along the outskirts of town, like the tackle shack we now occupy, only to abandon their old building to try anew in the city.

DD reluctantly suggested Travis and I go on a walk downtown, so I could familiarize myself with the Austin area. I mostly think she only said that to change the subject and try to lead me away from talking about our pasts and what I said during our trip to the junk tower.

We've been walking in silence for what feels like hours, just watching as people busy their lives away, completely ignorant to our presence among them. I walk behind Travis on the sidewalk, thinking about how normal this all seems. He looks like an everyday guy among the living. He might be dressed as though he's from a different time, but he still blends in as though he belongs with them. I could just see him on some shopping mission for gluten-free almond flour and organic honey that his wife enjoys with her tea. He walks with a purpose, ignoring the rest of the world just like they ignore us. Although unlike them, the illusion of Travis among the living dissipates the moment he walks straight through another couple who are walking in the opposite direction. He doesn't bother to move since he doesn't have to. They don't even flinch.

I guess that throws out any idea of figuring out some way of communicating with the living, as they can't even feel one of us pass through their bodies. I, on the other hand, quickly move out of the pair's way. It doesn't seem too unnatural, moving out of their way, as they are too engrossed in their own conversation to notice me even if I were alive.

"It's strange how everything seems so fast and so slow at the same time," I say, looking back at the couple moving past us so quickly, despite our walk here seeming hours long

"You'll get used to it," Travis replies, stopping in front of an old barber shop.

I all but run into him as he stares into the window. His eyes glass over as if he's in a trance for a long moment. I too look through the window, following his gaze into the barber shop. I watch as a wrinkled man laughs a deep, hardy laugh at something his younger client said. He waives around a silver pair of shears as if they could emphasize the meaning of whatever he was saying in reply to the boy in the chair.

The man goes back to cutting his client's hair and Travis rips his gaze away.

He looks down at me, tears swelling in his eyes that suddenly appear tired and lost.

"Some parts of this world you never get used to, though," he says, not bothering to make an excuse for his emotions like DD might have.

We start walking again.

"What was that?" I ask, having to run after him as his quick, long strides pull us away from the barber shop.

"Just a part of being a Wanderer," he replies sharply, dodging my question. "We should stop by the main market in the town square before we head back. There are usually a lot of Freshies there."

"Do you know that man," I ask, gesturing back toward the barber shop, ignoring his attempt to change the subject. "Who is he?"

"Please River, just let it go," he says wiping away more tears before they can fall from his eyes. It's then that I realize Travis, too, has been here a long time. The longing and far-off look in his eyes is the same as DD's. Neither of them seem to have a face that matches their true selves. Both of them feel the same confusion and longing for something missing that I feel. He looks down at me once again, begging me with his almost purple shaded eyes to not ask any more questions.

I take a deep breath and let it out slowly, nodding my head, agreeing to let it go for now. He sends me a lopsided grin before continuing about the market as if nothing happened.

"Sometimes other Wanderers will go there to watch people as well. It'd be good for you to learn how to discern the two from each other."

"When I first talked to DD, she made it seem like it might be dangerous to talk to other Wanderers," I say, reluctantly deciding to let him change the topic, knowing I'll still be receiving some answers about life as a Wanderer if he replies accordingly.

"Well, some Wanderers don't always have the best intentions, so that's partially true," he says, pausing to scan, what I assume to be, the entrance of the market. "What she's really worried about are the Freshies. A good rule of thumb is to stay away from other dead people if you're alone. Once you know someone's safe to talk to, then you're fine. Just don't wander off and talk to other ghosts on your own for a while."

"How do you know if someone's safe to talk to?"

"The biggest clue is when you don't get any strange feelings about them," he says, his body disappearing again as a living person passes through him, exiting the busy marketplace. He doesn't even flinch, as if having someone suddenly walk through you is the most ordinary thing in the world. He pauses again before continuing, his voice becoming a bit more solemn. "Although we don't have any solid memories from our waking lives, our consciousness can somehow be triggered by people or places that we used to know."

"Is that what happened earlier? At the barber shop," I say slowly, not wanting to upset him, but still curious.

He freezes again before turning his face away from me. "I get drawn there sometimes, but not all the time," he says, his voice dipping lower so that I almost can't hear him. "I come to the city often. It boggles my mind when I get these strange waves of emotion. It happens almost every time I pass by there. Sometimes I feel nothing at all, while other times I'll start uncontrollably laughing or crying. I don't know why though."

Is that going to happen to me? I suddenly feel a coolness in the air, almost as if it's surrounding just me. I don't like the idea of not being able to control myself, and worse, not knowing the cause of those intense emotions to overcome me.

I look out at the crowded grocery, with no one able to see me. A woman in her early thirties pushing her half-filled cart with her fit-throwing toddler sitting in the seat by her hands: his little legs flailing on the other side of the two leg holes of the cart as he cries in protest of not getting yogurt. A young teenage worker helping an old man reach for a box of uncooked pasta off the top shelf. A girl with a butterfly t-shirt trying to convince her exhausted mom to buy her a chocolaty cereal. A man yelling on the phone with his wife, staring intently at a pen-marked sticky note in utter confusion.

I feel my breath hitch in my throat, not wanting to be invisible. Wanting to be seen and a part of this scene somehow, I suddenly feel more lost than I did just moments ago.

No one cares about you.

"Hey," Travis snaps, bringing my attention back to him.

I stare at him, almost shocked by his presence, feeling confused but also glad to see him standing beside me.

"It'll be okay," he says sternly. His voice calms me down as he looks straight into my eyes, as if understanding what I was feeling just a second ago. What was that?

"It happens to all of us, but you won't be alone," he adds reassuringly, all the strange, anxious feelings I had a second ago completely disappearing. "DD and I will be able to help you through it."

I look down at his hands, touching my upper arms. I'm

surprised by the coolness coming from his calloused hands and the slight pinching of his metal ring on my skin. He's touching me. I look back up and meet his gaze.

He sees me. I'm not alone. My breathing slows and I start to feel safe again.

"Sorry, I don't know what happened," I start to say, but he cuts me off.

"Like I said, sometimes we start to get strange feelings because of our previous lives." He abruptly stands up straight, letting his arms fall back to his sides taking the coolness with him. "I don't really know what triggered you, but if you figure it out, try to stay away from it," he adds, as if I'm supposed to know what he means.

Part of me wants to object, wanting to know why DD and Travis both insist on staying away from anything that makes us feel, but I stop myself. I just nod my head curtly, like a child reluctantly submitting and obeying their parent, not really wanting to feel whatever that was again anytime soon.

"I didn't bring you here to explore the negative parts of Wanderer membership, but instead for some fun learning," Travis explains, his lopsided smirk sneaking back onto his face.

I look at him curiously, not sure if Travis's version of 'fun' is the same as mine, but I decide to follow him into the market anyway.

"You get to figure out which of the people in this room are living and which are dead!" he exclaims, seeming to do a complete one-eighty in personality, jumping and clapping his hands excitedly. "Bonus points if you can differentiate between the Freshies and the true Wanderers," he adds, his snarky attitude clearly marking its territory once again.

I look around the large store, the isle walls short enough

to see almost everyone inside. It appears everyone is doing typical things within a grocery store: shopping and minding their own business.

"How am I supposed to tell the difference? It's not like we all have giant signs over our heads saying, 'Hey, I'm a ghost!'" I state, waving my arms around, wiggling my fingers like DD did by the tower of junk.

"Look closer," he says, laughing at my ghost impression. "You see how you and I have blue skin?"

"Everything's blue." I deadpan, starting to think he might be messing with me instead of actually trying to help me.

"Look at the hue. Mine is different from yours."

"So what?" I look closer at the woman and her crying baby, noticing that they seem to have the same indigo coating as the rest of the scenery, not having their own bluish shade like Travis and I do. It's as if a bluish screen was placed over them and everything else in the world. I look back at Travis and notice that he is a deeper blue than the woman and her kid. It's almost as if the film layered over itself two or three more times when coating him before it covered the rest of the world. He smiles, taking note of my realization. He nods his head back toward the rest of the room, as if telling me to look again.

My eyes roam over the marketplace, eager to test out my new theory. Almost in an instant, my eyes catch onto the old man from before. What I thought was a teenage worker helping an old man reach some pasta was actually a worker restocking the shelves and an old man who doesn't seem to realize he's dead. His skin all but glows a light shade of blue, much closer to my arctic hue than Travis's deep indigo.

26

"He's a Freshie," I say, pointing at the old man in excitement.

I don't bother waiting for Travis's affirmation before letting my eyes search for the next victim. The little girl with the butterfly t-shirt seems to glow almost a dark grayish-blue and I realize she too is one of us.

"Is she a Wanderer since her skin is darker like yours and DD's?" I ask, a bit more uncertain of my discovery, gesturing to the little girl.

"That's a good guess, but no," Travis explains, running a hand through his hair. "I'm not really sure what causes the specific hues of blue each of us are painted with once we die, but they don't change once you see blue."

"Then how can you tell if someone is a Freshie or a Wanderer?"

"How they act. Freshies often try to interact with the living for a little while, not realizing they're dead," he says, shrugging as if it's obvious. "Usually, it takes another Wanderer to tell them the truth, or they become a Wanderer themselves with time. Believe it or not, but some people go crazy, obsessing over their past lives. Those are the Wanderers you need to look out for."

"How do you know if someone's going to become a Wanderer?"

He pauses, as if pondering over how to respond. "It's something you'll figure out the longer you're here. It's more of just an instinct, I guess." I look between the little girl and the old man and wonder whether they will become Wanderers like us.

"How do you determine whether you can trust another Wanderer or not?"

"That's a bit trickier," he replies, crouching down, folding his elbows over his knees as he sits on the title.

"Well then, how did you know that you could trust me," I ask, plopping down beside him, not letting him escape my question this time. "Maybe I'm dangerous?"

"You're harmless," he laughs deeply, tossing his head back dramatically, leaning on the palms of his hands and sticking his long legs out in front of him. "Besides the fact that DD brought you, which is an impressive feat, you give off a wave of innocent energy. It's almost sickening to stand around you," he says, pretending to gag as if reacting to the stench of me.

"DD does seem to be the overly cautious type, so I guess that would be enough," I reply, ignoring his stupid comments and dramatic gestures.

"You have no idea." he groans. "She freaks out at the slightest hints from our waking lives. She acts as if I'm one of those idiots who intentionally seeks out their past life."

"What would happen if you did? What's so bad about knowing?"

"Sorry, I didn't mean to get you to question that." Travis sighs. "It's probably for the best that you don't worry about it. Especially after both of us feeling the effects after just small hints from the past today."

I huff at his response, slightly irritated that he won't tell me, but also knowing that he won't budge if I push harder for an answer.

"We probably shouldn't mention the barber shop or your little episode to DD. She'll start to worry and—trust me— you don't want that."

"Fine, I won't tell her," I reply, still bugged about his dodgy behavior, but also knowing that telling DD would only make him less likely to tell me things in the future.

. . .

I watch the trees rustle as I walk down the gravel road toward the town. The wind sings past my ears, and I instinctively flinch, but it doesn't sting or slap me in the face like I thought it would. I guess that's a perk of being a ghost. It makes sense though. When I think about it, the only things I've been able to physically touch are other ghosts, like when Travis touched me. I stare down at the loose rocks beneath my feet and try to kick at one of the larger pebbles. It doesn't move. I look around to make sure Travis isn't lingering behind me to laugh at my feeble attempt of moving the rock, but there isn't anyone there.

I've decided to try my best at following DD's rules, not always sure of what or why they exist. It's not as if I wanted or liked the feelings I got from whatever happened at the market. Luckily, I haven't run into any issues or had any weird emotions since that day at the market. Travis said it was a bit of a fluke since we both experienced some sort of remnant haunting from our past lives. I decided to just take his word for it, not wanting to jinx anything.

DD and Travis have been so kind to me and have helped me as much as they can to adjust to my new normal. It's weird because I can tell this, being dead, isn't normal, but it also feels so natural at the same time. Part of me thinks it's because I can't remember anything about my past, but another part of me feels comfortable, like I'm at home with DD and Travis.

I look up at the few buildings ahead as the makeshift road becomes paved, and I can't help but wonder about where I might have ended up if DD never found me. Would I just be as confused as that old man at the market? Surely, I would have eventually put the pieces together that I was dead. Who knows how long that would've taken? What would I have done if I had a panic attack because I didn't know what was happening at the market and Travis wasn't there? Would I be all alone?

I'm taken out of my thoughts, hearing a high-pitched scream coming from up ahead of me. I snap my head upwards and see two young boys about DD's size running down a small hill with plastic swords. The one in front trips and rolls in the grass for a moment, staining his white pants green before popping back up and continuing to run. The little blonde boy behind him giggles, swinging his silver sword around in the air.

"Harrison and Noah, get back here!" a woman yells, stepping out of the driver's seat of her tan minivan. The boys ignore her, giggling even more each time their plastic swords smack against each other.

"Guys, Ms. Tonya said we aren't supposed to play with our props for the show. You're gonna get all of us in trouble!" a little girl in a sparkly-pink leotard yells down at the boys, mimicking the woman and crossing her arms over her chest. "And we're gonna be late if you don't get to class."

"We're coming," the blonde boy yells back, slamming his sword into the other boy's side.

"Now, Harrison," the woman says, her tone dipping lower, making the blonde boy groan. His arms fall limp to his sides and he rolls his eyes. The other boy relaxes a moment later. "Come on, boys. Sybil's right. You need to get to practice if you want to be in the show."

I watch as the boys slowly trudge up the hill, not able to contain my smile as I watch the whole scene unfold. I curiously follow them up the hill, feeling as though I need to follow them. Reaching the top of the hill, I'm able to fully see them heading into a gray stone building with large glass windows all along the front entrance. I instinctively start running toward the building, a sense of desperation taking over my body, almost as if I need to be inside that building. I all but sprint after the small children and the woman holding one of the giant glass doors open for them. I push my feet to move faster as the woman starts closing the door behind them once all the kids make it inside. I reach out for the black door handle, but my hand goes right through it, and I'm snapped back to reality.

I shake my head, rapidly blinking my eyes as I try for the handle again. My hand passes right through it once more. I look up and through the glass, watching the woman and the three kids walking down the long hallway to the last door on the left and reality hits me again. I'm a ghost. For some reason, I felt alive for a moment and must have forgotten what I am. I look down at my hands again, slowly moving to stick my right hand through the glass. As my hand passes through the glass, a warm feeling takes over my body, my hand tingling as if sparks were prickling up from my fingertips.

I quickly yank my hand back through the glass, staring down at it both shocked and amazed. What in the world was that?

I stare up at the lit-up sign above the building reading *Tonya's Dance* in cursive purple letters. The sign seems somehow familiar, drawing me in. Holy crap. This place must have been something important to me from my waking life. The realization hits me, and I start to feel a bit anxious. I haven't recognized anyone or had any negative feelings from here yet, so maybe it's not a bad thing that I'm here. I stick my hand through the glass, feeling the tingling sensation again.

I pull my hand out.

DD wouldn't approve if she found out I came here. Nothing has happened so far, apart from the strange tingling feeling when I stick my hand through the door. I want to go in, but I stop myself. What if something bad happens? What if I start getting that terrible feeling again, like at the market? There's no telling if that will happen though.

"Vaughn, please help your sister put on her shoes." another woman's voice calls out, pulling me away from my thoughts. I turn my head toward her voice, seeing a young boy and girl and a woman carrying boxes headed my way.

"Ughh, mom! Why can't she do it by herself?" the boy, who I'm assuming is Vaughn, groans, dramatically throwing his arms up in the air.

"Just help her. My hands are full," she snaps, passing through my body to get to the door. The woman from before opens the door for her and takes one of the boxes from her as they walk inside, leaving the children outside. I look around, surprised that the woman left her young kids outside by themselves.

I ignore the pull to go inside the studio, deciding there's no harm in watching the young dancers from the outside. DD and Travis don't need to know I was here. I let myself enjoy the moment.

I just watch as the little girl hoists herself up on a skinny wooden bench alongside the giant windows, kicking her feet out so her brother can help her put her shoes on. Vaughn just huffs, shoving a marked-up pink ballet slipper onto her foot.

"I know you can do this yourself, Emma," he says, shoving the other slipper onto the next foot. His reluctant assistance makes a smug smile tug on her face.

"Yeah, but it's fun to see you kneel before me like I'm the princess in the play," the little girl, Emma, says kicking her feet out again.

"You're not the princess, though. Sybil is," Vaughn snaps back, smirking and shoving her feet out of his face.

"S-so what!" she stutters, not able to come up with a comeback. I let out a small chuckle, the two of them reminding me of DD and Travis's bickering back at the tackle shack.

"Emma. Vaughn. Get in here!" a woman's muffled shout reverberates through the glass, and the two kids take off running through me and into the building. The building pulls at me again.

I should go. I'm not supposed to be here. DD and Travis are waiting for me back at the shack. They wouldn't want anything bad to happen to me, and I can't guarantee that nothing bad would happen if I went in there. I watch the kids scurry to the back of the hallway, walking into the same room as the others, wanting to follow them in there.

I don't let myself go in, slowly stepping away from the building. With each step, the studio's draw lessens and my decision to leave becomes easier and easier, until I'm back on the part of the road where it starts to become gravel and the urge to run back to the studio completely disappears.

Chapter 3

A Friend

I t feels like months have gone by and I never could bring myself to tell DD or Travis about the dance studio, but I can't get it out of my head. Part of me wants to ask them about the tingling feeling I got when my hand went through the door, but I don't want DD to freak out on me and forbid me from going back. I know she doesn't technically have any power over my actions, and I probably shouldn't go back there, but I still don't want to make her worry or piss her off. I haven't decided if I will go back or not, so I don't see any point in telling her about the studio if it might not be relevant to any future events anyway.

Sitting legs crisscrossed by the edge of the river, I run my hand through the wet dirt where the rushing water meets the shore, imagining what it'd be like to feel the muddy mixture on my fingertips. Would it be grainy and rough like sand or smoother and squishy? I lean my head against my palm, propping my arm up on my knee.

Ever since the studio incident, I've spent any alone time I have near the river, not wanting to feel any more weird

34

remnant sensations from my waking life. Travis usually
goes into town to people watch, which I've discovered can
be quite fun, but I'd rather not risk going alone. He doesn't
seem to be too concerned about it, though. DD, however,
rarely leaves the tackle shop. The only time she ever leaves
is once a week to go who-knows-where. She never lets
either of us go with her, typically getting irritated when we
ask her about it. It's strange. Most of the time, DD seems to
keep a level head, only really getting worked up over things
that have to do with discussing our waking lives. I can't
help but be curious if wherever she goes has to do with why
it's so terrible that we know anything about our waking
lives.

I wish I could say it didn't bother me, not knowing why
we can't investigate our waking lives. It's not that I don't
trust DD and Travis, but being completely in the dark
about their rules makes me feel like they don't trust me
enough to tell me why. What are they hiding? What could
be so bad that they feel the need to keep it from me? Or is it
really that they don't trust me?

I uncross my legs, laying out flat, not worrying about
getting my clothes muddy, knowing nothing will stick to me
since I'm dead and can't touch anything. I stare up at the
sky, the green sun mesmerizing. I close my eyes and imagine
what it would feel like to have the heat radiating on my
skin. It almost feels natural, and I can almost picture it
becoming a reality before the idea completely vanishes from
my mind. Everything feels empty. Like an ever-extending
void taking over my mind that I can't escape. I hate the
uneasy feeling, but I've grown used to it. Well, as used to it
as I can, knowing that it's just a part of being a Wanderer.

"River, there you are," DD says, pulling me away from
my thoughts.

Opening my eyes again, I see DD standing over me with an almost disappointed look on her face. What on earth could she have to bitch about now?

"What are you doing here? You know that you shouldn't come here," she says, looking at the river anxiously, as if she's expecting something to jump out of it and snatch us at any second.

"I come here all the time and nothing has ever happened," I tell her, propping myself up on my forearms again. "If anything, this place calms me down and helps me think."

She visually relaxes her shoulders, letting out a small breath as if that reassured her somehow. She gives me another disapproving look, pinching her lips together and glaring before taking a seat next to me. Hopefully, she's decided to let it go.

This is where we first met. It somehow feels like yesterday, yet so long ago at the same time. Travis named me River because DD found me here. Travis once said he was named after the lake nearby where DD found him.

"It's so stupid how something so trivial as to where we met could dictate the name you have for the rest of your death," I say, trying to start a conversation that doesn't have to do with her scolding me. "Why do we call you DD?" I ask, thinking she must have come up with her own name.

She laughs, a real laugh, throwing her head back and catching me off guard. She looks out at the water longingly, yet with a sense of contentment. It's like she's recovering an old, joyful memory.

"It's been a while since I really thought about him, but there was another Wanderer that lived in the tackle shop before Travis and I inhabited it," she states calmly, as if this isn't the most insightful thing she's ever told me about herself.

I turn to face her fully, both shocked and excited to hear about another Wanderer. I haven't really been able to talk to anyone other than DD and Travis since I died.

"Fill was a real dunderhead, much like Travis. It's probably why I brought Travis to the shop in the first place. They would've been two peas in a pod, and probably would have driven me mad," she says, not able to contain her smile. "We weren't together long, but Fill made me feel like I'd be okay in this purgatory."

"So, Fill named you then?" I ask, not able to contain it anymore.

"Yeah. He was a bit cynical, naming me Dumpster Diver since that's where he found me." she chuckles at the memory, shaking her head.

I instantly and visibly flinch at the concept. I look at DD almost regretfully, filled with a sudden sadness at the realization that not only was she just a small child when she died, but that her body was put in a dumpster. My mind races with the possibilities of what that means for her poor waking life's death. The most obvious conclusion is that she was killed and dumped in a dumpster, left to rot after her life was taken from her. She must realize that too, but she's laughing.

"He was at least kind enough to not let me look and see my waking life's body. Who knows what that would've triggered in my memories," she jokes, sounding more like Travis as she displaces her trauma with humor.

I want to ask her if she's okay, and if she truly understands what she's saying about her waking life's end. She turns to me, and for once I see the truth. DD may act like an old woman with years of life experience, but inside she is a lost and hurt child whose life was taken too soon. As she looks me in the eyes, I see a vulnerability I've never seen from her before, begging me not to ask any questions for once.

I fight the curiosity inside me, not wanting to push her, realizing that telling me this much was already a lot for her. I silently thank her.

"Where is Fill now? I'd love to meet another Wanderer," I say, trying to veer the conversation in a different direction.

She grimaces and turns away. Shit. Maybe that might not have been the best question to ask next.

"He's not with us anymore," she says sternly, throwing up her walls again and returning to her usual composed nature.

I let out a deep sigh, knowing my window of questioning is officially closed off. I wrap my arms around my shins and lean my cheeks between my knees so that I don't have to face her. It's awkwardly quiet for a while. I feel bad for accidentally pushing her to close up again, but I can't help but feel dejected, knowing she doesn't trust me enough to tell me more about Fill or the in-between. Why won't she just tell me? She's so uptight and strict about her rules all the time! The one moment I think she's finally opening up and she shuts me out. I can't even get Travis to tell me anything.

I let out a small chuckle of disbelief, standing up abruptly. DD opens her mouth to say something, but I wave her off with my hand, too ticked off to listen to anything she has to say now. It's not like she's going to answer any of my questions. I can't believe I was feeling bad for her a moment ago. I don't look back at her as I walk away, determined to find the answers to my questions on my own.

. . .

I march up the gravel road toward Tonya's dance studio with more confidence than I've had since dying the large windows and gray stone walls giving off an almost warmth as I get closer. Who knows if I had much confidence during my waking life? All I know is that I'm drawn here for a reason. If DD and Travis want me to follow their rules, then they should tell me why these rules are in place. Since they won't tell me, I'm going to find out for myself.

As I approach the gray stone building, I start to feel the same pull toward the glass door I felt previously, my nervousness instantly returning as if the universe is trying to check me and put me back in place. I pause before the black handle, momentarily questioning if this is a good idea or not. DD and Travis seem to care about me and must have these rules for a reason. There has got to be consequences to acting on this pull, or they wouldn't have warned me about the draw.

You know what? Fuck the consequences. What's the worst that could happen? I'm already dead.

I go to grab the handle, my hand passing right through it. Right, I'm dead. I slip my hand through the glass, the familiar tingling sensation consuming my hand, forcing me to take an involuntary breath. Even though I knew it would happen, the warmth that surrounds me is still shocking as I push my whole arm through the door.

"If you're going to go in, just do it," a deep voice calls out from behind me.

I quickly drop my arm down in surprise, the tingling feeling subsiding as I step away from the door. Behind me stands a man with soft features, thinning grayish-blue hair, and crinkles around his eyes. By the royal blue tint to his

39

flesh, I am easily able to acknowledge him as a member of the dead. At first glance, I'd think he was just passing through, but something in his demeanor tells me otherwise.

I can't help but think that Travis would be proud of my detective skills, but now doesn't really seem to be the time to give myself a pat on the back.

"I don't want to make any promises, but I don't think this specific place will cause you too much harm if you want to go in. Especially since we are the only ones 'like us' around here," the man says, holding out his arms, his palms face forward as if trying to indicate his innocent intentions.

I stare at the man completely stunned, not knowing what to say, as he's the first person, other than DD and Travis, that I am able to have an actual conversation with. Thankfully, this conversation doesn't seem to involve me explaining someone's state of being among the dead to them, which is nice. Although, those conversations might seem less daunting than this one seems. DD or Travis are almost always with me, and I'm really wishing they were here to do most of the talking right now.

The man stares back at me patiently, tilting his head to the side, seeming slightly amused by my confusion and shock before deciding to speak again. "I saw you last time you came, but I didn't want to startle you. It seemed like your first time experiencing the draw. The Blue can be confusing at times, but once you're here long enough you'll understand the way things function and why. It's just part of the process."

"The Blue?" I question, my mouth not able to form complete sentences.

"Ah... That's just what I call this place." he shrugs, scratching the back of his head. "I don't know what else to call it. Everything here is blue, so I thought it made sense."

"So, you're a Wanderer," I conclude, letting a choppy laugh slip through my lips, realizing that the old man isn't a threat and I was just letting DD's paranoia get to me. If anything, he is just like me. I register his confusion at the term. He looks about how I did a moment ago. "That's just what my friends and I call people stuck in the in-between, or, well, the Blue, as you call it. Ya know, since we all just kinda wander."

He lets out a hearty laugh, not seeming in the slightest as cautious toward me as I was toward him a moment ago.

"I like it. Yeah, I'm a Wanderer then."

"Are you also drawn to this place? Does it mean something?" I ask, gesturing back to the studio with a wave of my hand, reminded of the reason I decided to come here.

"No, I just enjoy watching the youngsters working hard at something that they enjoy doing," he replies, a soft smile forming on his face as his gaze drifts toward the kids practicing in the window leading to the studio by the door.

I walk over to get a better look, the two of us watching as a group of four boys and four girls line up along either side of the barre in the center of the room. All of them are standing upright, awaiting instruction.

"It's fun watching them grow and figure out who they are. This group has been coming since they were toddlers. They are about to start middle school now, which is usually when they decide to quit or get serious about their dance careers."

I look closer at the dancers, realizing they are the same kids I saw last time I came to the studio. I notice the siblings first, their long noses and round deep-set eyes looking almost identical, their similarities stopping there. The blonde boy's hair is much longer now, tied up in a tight bun like the rest of the girls in the room. The boy he was playing with looks almost the same, standing at a smaller stature than the rest of the boys in the room. The little girl in the sparkly leotard, who had sassed the boys before, now stands at the front of the class barely able to hide her smug look. She was obviously chosen to show the class how to do a specific step by the instructor. It didn't feel like that much time had passed, but they are much older than the first time I saw them. There are a few new faces I don't recognize, but the five kids I watched play and torment each other last time are definitely the same kids in the studio.

"I thought you might recognize them," the old man chimes in, smiling brighter than before. "They've all gotten so close, coming here each day. Florence, the girl with the mousy brown hair is the newest to the group, but she and Avery have quickly become good friends."

"Which one is Avery?" I find myself asking, instantly sucked into their lives.

"She's the smaller, tan one with the thick, black hair," he explains, pointing, seeming just as excited as I am.

I'm not sure why, but I want to know everything about them. I feel suddenly engrossed by the idea of supporting them, knowing about their hopes and dreams, wanting to see them succeed. Everything I was worried about a second ago seems meaningless compared to the potential these kids have.

"Emerson is the other boy at the back of the class. He's newer to the group too. I don't think he was here when you came, but I can't remember," the man continues, scrunching his eyebrows together, looking at me for confirmation.

"I don't think he was, but I also didn't go inside to watch the classes or anything," I say, pausing, remembering why I'm here in the first place. "I'm not supposed to go in there."

"I don't think there will be anything too triggering for you here anymore, if there ever was at all," he says casually.

I snap my head in his direction, confused as to how he would know that.

"I've been coming here for a while now and I've never seen you. If this place was important to you when you were alive, then you must have been alive a long time ago. Definitely long enough for anyone close to you to be dead or long gone by now. Most people stop dancing here when they look about your age, and the owner changed just before you came last time, so the teachers probably aren't the same either."

"So, that means I'm just drawn here because it's a place that I frequented," I say, questioning whether or not that is enough to trigger whatever DD and Travis are so afraid of.

"Again, I can't guarantee that nothing will happen, but I've never seen a Wanderer, as you call us, go berserk after returning to a place from their time among the living," he says, walking through the window and into the studio.

I stand there, frozen and hesitating, as the unknown potential consequences of following him in creep into my mind again. What if something crazy starts happening? What if I get struck by lightning the moment I step through the glass? What if it hurts? But then again, what if nothing happens?

The dancers start lining up to attempt the move the smug girl demonstrated across the floor and I roll my shoulders back, taking in a deep breath. What if the old man is right? Fed up with the uncertainty, determined to answer my own questions from here on out, I take the step toward the glass.

Chapter 4

Names

The room feels cold. Not telling DD and Travis about the old man the second I got here is proving more difficult than I initially thought it'd be. The silence within these white walls making me feel as though I'm losing my mind. I may be irritated with DD at the moment, but the awkward silent treatment between the two of us has been deafening. If the only conversation I'm able to have is one of Travis's 'hot boy' ramblings he goes on every time he sees a minorly attractive guy, then I'll find a way to unalive myself again.

"I met another Wanderer," I spit out, not able to hold it in anymore. Despite the fact the secret has been eating at my soul so much that I would probably have severe stomach pains if I were alive, I want to set the precedent that I won't keep major and important secrets from them, despite them not doing the same for me. Obviously, I don't plan to tell them all my secrets, but I don't want to be a complete hypocrite.

"What? When?" Travis asks, jumping up off the

cement floor, suddenly more interested in what I have to say than adjusting his collar and slacks, preparing for another night on the town.

I don't completely face her, but I can sense DD's interest from out of the corner of my eye as she subtly peers her head through the doorframe into the main area of the shop.

"A couple weeks ago," I say nonchalantly, shrugging my shoulders and inadvertently making my way toward the screen door, trying to make it seem like it wasn't as big of a deal to me as it was. "I was just walking around, and he started talking to me while I was people watching," I explain further, telling half the truth.

"Well, what was he like? Was he cute?" Travis asks, lowering his voice seductively, following me outside excitedly as if I told him Elvis was waiting for him at the bottom of the hill.

"If you call a wrinkly old man cute, then sure." I let out a small laugh, playfully slapping his arm as he pouts.

"I was just joking. I mean most of the wanderers we see are like those creepy hairless cats anyway. I was just being hopeful," he replies, rolling his eyes and cocking his hip to the side. "But seriously, what happened?"

"We just talked for a bit." I shrug, trying to recall our conversation without giving too much away. "We talked about people watching, since that's what I was doing when he snuck up on me."

"He snuck up on you?" DD all but snaps the question, popping her head out of the wall making her look like a taxidermied deer head, finally breaking her silence, her worrying, motherly self takes the reins.

"Yeah, but I'm fine," I say, brushing her off, not wanting

the conversation to swerve into one of her lectures. "He said he calls the in-between 'the Blue.' Ya know, since everything here has that blueish tint? I thought it was kinda clever."

"That is a good name for it." Travis snorts, looking between DD and me. "Why didn't we ever think of a name for where we are?"

"I guess I just always called it the in-between, since we are sort of stuck in between the realms of the living and the dead," I say, looking back toward DD for a response. "But I think I like the Blue more."

"You know, I just call it what it is. Purgatory," DD says, practically glaring at Travis as her body passes completely through the rotting paneled wall.

"Purgatory?" I question, not really sure what she means. "Like hell on earth?"

"No, Purgatory is more a place where you go before reaching heaven," she explains, walking passed Travis, moving closer to where I'm standing at the base of the grassy hill. "It's where you are able to let go of your earthly tethers and spend a bit more time reflecting and atoning for your sins and transgressions before joining Jesus in heaven. I like to think of it like some of us just needed a little extra time to cook in Purgatory in order to be ready enough for God in heaven."

"Oh," I pause, not really knowing what to say as all three of us go quiet.

I turn to Travis, hoping he'll fill the silence like usual, only for him to suddenly be overly interested in the rotting yellow siding on another abandoned building we're walking past as we approach the more civilized area away from the main lake. The one time the loudmouth decided to shut up is when I finally need him to help me reignite communications with DD.

"I guess I haven't really thought of going somewhere else," I say, glancing awkwardly between DD and a random tree branch hanging a little too low, making me duck beneath it as we pass by. "The idea of going somewhere else doesn't seem too bad though."

DD all but lights up at my statement, not noticing my discomfort. She jumps a bit as she passes through the tree trunk, her blonde curls stilling in the air as if they are immune to gravity. It's not often that I've seen DD appear so excited about something, but then again, she's never talked to me directly about any sort of belief system before.

The concept of heaven seems wonderful, but I don't have a ton of hope that we will be able to get there even if it does exist. I mean, I thought it'd be rude to ask the exact time, but Travis and DD have been stuck here for who knows how long. Any hope for me to move on to elsewhere seems like a pipe dream, but I don't want to be the one to squash her dreams.

"Alright DD, that's enough evangelization for the day," Travis says, dragging out his words as if he were talking to a someone the age DD appears to be.

Her face instantly falls, no doubt about whether or not she is glaring at him now.

"Just because you don't understand something doesn't mean that you have to ruin a good thing for River," DD snaps, her eyes turning inferno quicker that I'd thought to be possible from her previous elated state.

Oh shit.

"It's not that I don't understand; it's the fact that no one wants to listen to you shoving your religion down their throats when clearly your argument is flawed," he yells, throwing his hands around in the air for emphasis.

"She asked!" she yells back, waving her hand in my direction, matching Travis's energy.

I take a step back, wishing their argument could evaporate me so it can't change directions and aim toward me. I try to think of ways to change the topic, but their argument just turns into a screaming match and no interjection from me would stop it. I can't help but compare myself to a small child with divorced parents who are fighting for custody. We are like a makeshift family of sorts, all of us living together and caring for each other in our own ways. It's just mom and dad fighting in their typical dysfunctional way. I try not to laugh at the thought, not wanting to let DD or Travis think I'm laughing at them even though I am in a way.

"Whatever! Be damned for all I care! It's not my problem." DD scoffs, shaking her head, making her blonde curls fly around her as she turns to storm away from us, back toward the tackle shack.

"Okay, dramatic much," Travis quips, rolling his eyes before turning to face me. "Sorry about that."

"Is this a recurring topic of discussion?" I inquire, looking over his shoulder, hoping not to see a fuming DD still standing behind us. Lucky for me, she stormed herself completely out of earshot, leaving the two of us between a string of abandoned buildings and the backside of a grocery store at the real start of the town.

"She's always talking about us 'atoning for our sins' and 'moving on to salvation,' but I think it's just rude to give people false hope. It's one thing if she wants to stay delusional, but another to force her delusions onto other people."

"She sure seems to believe it," I say softly, not wanting to start a fight with him too.

"That's true." he sighs, playing with the gold ring on his pinky finger, looking back toward the trail we came from. "I feel bad for putting her down, but I just can't handle her going on and on about a future that doesn't make any sense. If what she's saying is true, then her material sins as a six-year-old were bad enough for her to be stuck here for almost a century at this point. Meanwhile, other old, wet rags that pass through here are only here for what? A week tops? That doesn't add up."

"There may be flaws in her logic, but do you really want to squash her hope for something else?" I don't bother to add the fact that she admits the way other people are able to move on is triggered by their waking bodies being put to rest, not wanting to fuel the fire any further. "I wish I could believe that the Blue is just a temporary state like Purgatory. I mean, the concept of moving on to somewhere better and beautiful would be motivation enough to get through the day. Why would you want to ruin that for her?"

"I would rather face reality than be ignorant," he says with a huff.

"Ignorance is bliss, right?" I say, letting out a small chuckle, running a hand through my hair.

"Sorry, this got out of hand." Travis sighs, facing me fully. "You were telling us about a new friend. I didn't mean to take over the conversation."

I open my mouth to tell him about the old man when a wave of pressure pushes me toward Travis and my body suddenly feels like television static. Wrapping my arms around myself as if rubbing them will make the feeling disperse, I glance up at Travis to see his eyes widening, realizing something I can't quite place. He quickly tackles me to the ground like a pro footballer, somehow pinning me in place with his lanky arms so that I can't get up off the grass.

"What giv-," I start to yell but he cuts me off, slapping his large hand over my mouth, his eyes begging me to stop talking. I do as he says, knowing I'm going to have to get an explanation from him later when the tingling feeling consuming my body only worsens, making me feel as though I'm about to throw up. I try to sit up to catch a glace at what could be causing this, but I'm firmly reminded not to move by Travis's entire bodyweight holding me stiffly in place.

"JamieandLauren–Compactor–Betrayed–Revenge– OhItHurts–JamiePlease–   LaurenHelpMeStop–Betrayed– BeesNeedFreeingDamnit–ItHurtsJamie–PleaseStop–Free– MeLauren–Hurts," a strangled voice starts yelling from inside the yellow painted building, making Travis's entire body tense above me. My chest tightens as I look to meet Travis's panicked eyes, still confused but my fingers squeezing around the loose fabric of his suit sleeves. I slowly let my eyes move upward to Travis's scrunched forehead, to the edge of his receding hairline, then daring to look beyond to the now deep purple air around us. My stomach unconsciously clenches as I let my gaze drift toward the window above us, a slightly reddish glow illuminating from inside. Since dying, I've never been able to see any other real colors that weren't tainted by the Blue. It didn't occur to me before to long for any other colors, for more, but the feeling of seeing deep purple and red only make the bile in my throat and the itching within my skin burn more intently. My nails dig into the scratchy fabric beneath them tightly and I try to pull Travis's body closer to me.

I stare up at the angled edge of the windowsill, as a chill seems to radiate off the black PVC stone. Small, burgundy-colored fingers wrap around the edge and the yelling gibberish gets louder. Fear pulses through my veins as I stare up at the hand, not able to pull my gaze from the remnants of molding blue skin stuck beneath its jagged fingernails. Part of me wants to try and help this poor creature, begging for help, but the familiar hue of the dead skin between its claw like fingers prevents me from moving. A loud inhuman shriek echoes from above, making both Travis and I jolt from the sound. It takes every ounce of self-control to keep myself from letting out a sob, tears streaking toward my ears as I bite down on my lips. I silently plead for the thing to go away, so that we can escape back to DD and the safety of the tackle shack.

The thing lets out another high-pitched screech, sounding almost pained before they remove their hand from the window, backing away from us. Travis doesn't hesitate to lift me up off him and the ground, my arms and legs wrapping around him like I was a child, not able to do anything else as he charges back toward anywhere but here. His feet move so quickly one might have thought he was a track star in his youth, pushing past many run-down houses and scraggily trees. It's only when we get to the base of the grassy hill close to the tackle shack that he finally slows to put me down.

"What on earth was that," I say, slightly stuttering, making me realize my body is still shaking.

"That is the reason DD says to stay away from other Wanderers," Travis says, frantically looking back toward the path we just came from, as if making sure that thing didn't follow us.

"That 'thing' was a Wanderer," I half yell, not sure what to make of this information. There's no way that thing could be anything like us. Their aura alone, practically forced the non-existing shit out of my rectum.

"That 'thing' is why DD always worrying about us looking into our pasts," Travis says, twisting his ring around his finger again, not taking his eyes off the path. "Apparently she knew someone who turned into a Shell like that after he learned about who he was in his waking life. She's wigged out about anything involving our waking lives ever since."

"Do you think it saw us," I ask, glancing in the same direction as Travis, not knowing if I want the answer or what it may entail.

"I think we are safe for now. Let's not tell DD about what happened today. I don't want her to worry, especially since I already pissed her off before we ran into the Shell."

I just nod my head, agreeing, and not knowing what else to say.

"Damn it, Noah," Sybil snaps, shoving his hands off her waist and turning to face him. "If you want me to help you practice your lifts, you need to at least get your grip right so that I don't get hurt."

"Sorry, I know, sorry," Noah replies under his breath, bowing his head submissively as Vaughn snickers from the other side of the room.

It being so late, I didn't think anyone would be in the studio. I was happily surprised to see the three of them working on a new lift they learned last week in class. It's for a specific competition they are joining in the spring. They've been doing more competitions now that they are getting older. It's exciting to see them not just getting better each time I come to visit, but to also see their dedication and passion for the sport grow.

I wanted to get away from DD and Travis for a while. I came to the studio hoping to clear my head and then I found the trio. I'm not sure what it is about these kids, but they always seem to distract me from my deathly reality. Tonight is no different, and I gladly welcome the distraction.

"I swear if I get injured because I decided to help you out, I will throw a major bitch fit," she huffs, rubbing her ankles as if she were already feeling the effects of an oncoming injury. "Vaughn, please help me show him how to do this correctly."

Vaughn pops up off the wall he was leaning against, his smile widening as he replaces Noah's spot next to Sybil. He rolls his shoulders back, flexing his muscles when he makes eye contact with Sybil, as if he's trying to look macho for the young girl still a few inches taller than him. Sybil just ignores him, preparing to initiate the lift again.

"Oh, to be young and learning how love stings," the old man says, smiling softly at the trio.

I feel the smile instantly spread across my face the moment I see him, having wanted to talk to him for weeks. For some reason, I thought he'd just always be here, like a simulated non-player character in a videogame, awaiting my arrival. However, that's not the case. I go to hug him, over-taken by my excitement and ignoring the fact that we've only really met once before. He chuckles, accepting my hug. I'm not sure what it is about him, but I feel this connection that differs from the one I get when I'm around DD or Travis. It's not a draw-like connection that has to do with our waking lives, but more of a sense of comradery and life/death understanding between us.

"It's been a while, but you seem to be doing much

better." he returns my smile, pulling back and gesturing to the studio walls around us. "You came in all by yourself this time."

"Ha ha," I say, brushing him off. "I'm still not used to the tingly feeling I get while I'm in here though."

"It's electrifying, right?" he asks, tapping his swollen fingers on his arm as if to show his meaning.

I nod, tracing my own fingers up my pale arms. He's right. It really is like electricity is running through my veins. I don't think I've ever been on drugs during my waking life, but I'm sure this is what it'd feel like. Complete bliss. My mind races every time I'm here and everything seems more vivid, like another enhanced filter is placed over the blue one, making the details and colors of things clearer and sounds crisper and more beautiful. If this is the madness Travis was talking about, then I think he might be misinformed or overreacting. Part of me wants to ask the old man about the Shells, but I also don't want him to confirm everything Travis said. I don't want a reason to not come back here.

Wow. I do want to keep coming here. I want to keep watching the dancers grow and talk with the old man. The realization takes me aback for a moment, creating an awkward pause between the old man and myself.

"I was thinking about you a lot lately and realized I forgot to introduce myself and ask for your name," I say, running a hand through my hair, trying to start the conversation again. "I'm River, by the way," I add, feeling bad about not doing this earlier.

"Well, it's nice to meet you, River. That's a lovely name," he says, smiling at my nervousness. "I don't remember my name, and I don't usually talk to people enough to need one, so I guess I don't have one." He shrugs, seeming unbothered while watching the trio practice their lifts again.

"You don't have a name?" I ask, shocked at the revelation. I guess that makes sense, since I didn't remember my name and didn't have one until Travis named me River. I think back to that day, remembering how anxious it made me feel, not having a name. I doubt the old man is truly unbothered by it. "Do you think I could give you a name?" I ask the question before I have a chance to really think about it. That's so stupid. Why would he want me to give him a name? He's been in the Blue longer than me and probably doesn't care. Why would he want a girl he just met to give him something so importantly unimportant?

"That'd be very kind of you." he beams, making all my worries fade away. "It'd be nice to have someone call you by something that is your own and given to you so deliberately."

I smile back at him, both nervous and excited to come up with a name for him. He seems so happy about having a name, but nothing comes to mind right away. I don't want to give him a boring name or something lame too hastily. "Can you give me a while, though? I wanna take my time with it."

"That's considerate of you," he says, nodding his head. "If I'm going to be stuck with it for the rest of eternity, it might as well be a good one."

"Jesus Christ, Noah!" Sybil yells, grabbing our attention again. "You're such a fuck up. You seriously hurt my waist! You're totally manhandling me."

"Dude, you need to use your plié more. It's not all about the arms," Vaughn adds, trying to defuse the situation. "You'll get it. Don't worry too much."

Sybil doesn't seem to care about his efforts, bending

down to pick up her purple duffle bag near the large mirror. "He can get it on his own because I'm done risking my own health to teach him."

"Come on, Sybil. Don't be like that," Vaughn says, running after her exiting form.

Their voices disappear down the hallway and the old man and I are left alone with Noah in the studio. We both stand silently as he runs his thin fingers through his dark, floppy hair. I find myself holding my breath, as if Noah could hear me if I exhaled too loudly. I take a moment to watch him as he stares at his reflection in the mirror, tears pooling in his eyes.

He moves slowly at first, his arms elegantly floating in a rhythmic motion. It takes me a moment to recognize the choreography. It's from their piece for the competition, but not Noah's part. Instead, I recognize the movements to be Vaughn's part, which is the lead male part that compliments Sybil's leading role. His movements captivate me in a way that I don't usually feel during their practices. His precision is anything but flawless but the emotion pulsating through his body is enchanting. His movements aren't the same as they usually are in class. This is different. At this moment, he is different. He isn't just going through the motions of how someone else wants it to be; he's dancing how he sees it. He's free. He isn't just the dance, but instead the dance is him. It's beautiful.

"Wow, that kid can move," I hear the old man say, neither of us taking our eyes off Noah. "He's like Pierre meets ballet."

I let out a small laugh at the idea, still entranced by Noah's dancing. He's right, though. He does move more like a ballroom dancer than a ballet dancer.

The echoing of a door slamming from the hallway

makes all of us jump, and Noah stops dancing. "Sorry, dude," Vaughn's voice calls out from the hallway, his steps getting louder as he approaches. "She said she won't help anymore, and then she left."

"It's fine." Noah sighs, clearly upset by the news. "It's not like I am strong enough to do lifts anyway. I don't think practicing over and over is going to fix my body."

"Dude, you just need to hit the gym more," Vaughn says, wrapping his arm around him and flexing his free bicep for emphasis. "Harrison and I go every morning before school. You should join us."

"It's tough being a boy at that age," the old man says, scratching the back of his head. "I see it all the time. The societal pressures to look a certain way, be strong, and not show weakness ruins the purities of youthfulness."

"But he's just a late bloomer! He'll grow like the others. He just hasn't hit puberty yet," I add, somehow feeling as though I need to defend Noah. His skills as a dancer are so natural and lovely. I'm sure he just needs to grow into himself and he will be one of the best dancers in the world.

"That's just life, though," the old man says, tilting his head as he looks at me and smiles. "One of my favorite parts of watching the living is seeing how they handle their struggles and learn from them. If life was easy, then what would be the point?"

I take a moment to really think about what he said, realizing that he's right. The only thing that bothers me with that reality is what that means for us: the dead. We are just frozen in time, with no real meaning or purpose. "What are we supposed to do now? Just watch them?"

His smile just widens at my response and he stares into my eyes with a sort of glint in his, somehow following my train of thought. "Watch and marvel."

I can't help but contain my laughter at the simplicity of his answer, but also at the completely carefree look on his face as he says it. "Watch and marvel? I guess that's a good death motto." I then realized that's a perfect name for him. "How about Marvel, then?"

"I'm sorry?" he questions, not following anymore. "For your name in the Blue? How about I call you Marvel?"

"I like it," he says, grinning back at me.

Chapter 5

Motivation

I lean back on my elbows, sticking my feet out, as Travis goes on about some famous baseball player he saw in town. I absentmindedly run my fingers through the tall blades of grass beside me, not bothering to feign fascination as I tune out of the conversation. I've felt better since I told Travis and DD about Marvel, even though they don't realize that I've gone back to see him again. I still haven't told them about the dance studio, and I'm not sure if I ever will, despite how guilty I feel about going there and keeping secrets from them.

"Ughh! He was so hot!" Travis all but yells, pulling my attention back to him as he huffs dramatically next to me. "DD, you're just a prude. Riv, I know you would've thought he was just gorg too. Maybe you could go with me next time and we can ogle some hot guys at the club? I heard about this new one downtown that's supposed to be super fun."

"Why go if you can't even talk to anyone?" DD says, waving her hand as if dismissing the idea. "Even if you did run into another Wanderer, they are usually obnoxious.

Besides, you can't even have a normal conversation over all the loud music."

"I've never been to a club," I say, trying to prevent an argument and change the subject, although I'm not really sure if I want to go into town again. I'm not completely closed off to the idea, but all the strange feelings I got last time I went into town made me feel anxious. "I mean, it's not like I'd remember if I had or not," I add realizing they would've already known about most of my experiences post death.

I've probably gone to a club before. I look to be the right legal age. It sounds fun to me now, so it probably sounded fun to me when I was alive too. There are probably so many things I've experienced before and not realized it. I can't help but think there are so many things that I have reexperiencing for the first time again with out realizing it. Were my reactions in the past different or the same or did the order in which I experience things and how I experience them shape my other choices and desires when I experienced other things?

"Well then, we have to go! DD, you in?" Travis asks, jumping back up off the grass, looking over at DD with what you could only call pleading hopefulness in his eyes.

"I guess we can go, but not today," DD says, standing and brushing the nonexistent dust off her dress.

"Why not? It's a Saturday and the best night to go." Travis pouts, as she turns to walk back inside the shop.

"I have church in the morning and don't want to accidentally miss it," she replies curtly, as if it were obvious. "We can go next Friday."

"Fine," he groans before turning to me, grinning like a wild cat and wiggling his eyebrows like a small child would.

I shake my head, smirking back at him, starting to feel

excited about going somewhere fun with both of them. I can't believe DD agreed to go, but also wonder if part of the reason for her lack of protest is her attempt to support Travis and make up for their fight a few weeks ago.

It hits me then, and I process all of what she said. I twist my head to look at her, wanting to ask her about it. Seeing as she's always so adamant about us not going into town alone, I'm shocked to find out she's going to church, and apparently that she goes regularly. Why hasn't she said anything about it before?

I open my mouth to ask how often she goes to the church, but I stop myself. She probably won't tell me the truth if I ask, so I shouldn't bother. She never answers any of my questions, so why would she now?

I'm not sure what outer force finally pushed me to follow DD to the cathedral. Whether it was this "God" she goes on and on about or if it was just my ceaseless curiosity, I'm here. Standing outside the daunting, wooden double doors, I start to regret following her. Although I know the crowd around me can't see me, I feel their eyes consuming me, screaming out to me that 'I don't belong.' The place itself is massive. If it weren't for the sculped angels, made to blow into twisted horns, flanking the main doors and a steeple at the highest point of the building, one might have mistaken it for a castle from the Middle Ages. People gather around the manicured front courtyard, dressed in tea length dresses or slacks, mingling amongst each other, catching up on their day to day lives. A little boy and girl giggle as they run by me and around their mother, who is fruitlessly trying to keep them settled whilst not breaking away from her conversation with some older woman who works at the church. Another elderly couple help each other over the curb, holding hands as they move from the street to the sidewalk. Everyone looks so happy, but I can't help the pit forming in my stomach, feeling as though they wouldn't accept me if I were to follow them inside.

DD has no problems easily transforming into a lemming as she walks into the limestone dungeon. I quickly lose sight of her pink dress in the crowd, making me feel even more like an outsider. I want to run away or scream for DD to come find me, but I know that'll only cause more problems for me later. I really don't need another scolding from DD about the dangers of the waking world or how rude it is to follow someone without their knowledge.

"You gonna just stand outside the door like an afternoon farmer or are you gonna go in?" Travis's deep voice mocks from behind me. I jump and whip my head around, not expecting him to have followed me considering how he feels about churches.

"What are you doing here?" I ask him, trying my best to sound bored rather than exposing how nervous I am.

"I may hate these bible beaters, but I couldn't let my sweet Riv go in on her own, now, could I?" He jokes, slinging a lanky arm around my shoulders, playfully pulling me close and smiling.

I try my best to smile back, but his dark eyes whisper to me, telling me he's just as terrified as I am. For the few years I've been with Travis, he's always seemed so sure of himself, taking most things about death in stride or as a joke. He's never told me, but I've seen the way his eyes glaze over when DD talks about the church or her theories on the in-between being some form of purgatory. I know not to push him and just let myself feel the warmth that comes from him being here to support me and my curiosity.

We walk closer to the giant wooden doors, into the crowd of followers. We walk silently past many families, not surprised when none of them seem affected by our presence. I don't know what I was thinking, but I thought maybe we could be recognized by the living in such a sacred and magical place. That's just my hope taking though. I feel Travis tense up, and both of us stop just before the main entrance.

"I don't know why DD comes here. It smells like old people," he jokes, pinching his nose and fake gagging, as if he doesn't live in a rotting, fish-smelling tackle shack in the middle of nowhere.

A snort slips out of my nose, his antics effectively calming me down enough to do this. "Let's get inside and maybe it'll smell better, sweet princess," I reply, sarcasm seeping into my tone. I pull him by the arm before he can retort, the two of us moving through the thick doors and into the lemming pool.

Stepping into the cathedral, I'm instantly stunned by its beauty. The limestone walls are adorned with hand woven tapestries that appear to be centuries old, although they were probably made to only look that way. The main sanctuary is lit by massive crystal chandeliers and symmetrical elongated arched windows on either side of the rows of pews. The pews almost point anyone walking in to face the giant, stained-glass rose window behind the altar. The organist starts playing as the lemmings file into their seats. The pastor, dressed in long white robes and a funny looking hat, makes his way to the altar. The old man puts his hand in the air, his fingers outstretched and filled with energy, reminding me of Noah's dance. The church falls into a practiced silence. He starts singing in a language unfamiliar to me, and the lemmings singing back to him like a swarm of bees instinctly responding to their queen. I search the crowd, finding DD standing near the front with a few other Wanderers I've never seen before.

I gasp, quickly turning to point them out to Travis as well. He shushes me, placing a hand over my mouth before I can get a word out, not wanting to call attention to us. I return my gaze and nod in understanding. He sees them too. By the look on his face, it doesn't seem like he knew about them either. It's not unusual for DD to not tell me things, but DD and Travis have been together for a lot longer. This time it seems DD kept both of us in the dark.

How come she's never told us about them? I look back, counting six other Wanderers whom she seems rather familiar with. Her skin seems to almost glow a lilac color as she shakes their hands in welcome. A pit forms in my stomach. I hate the fact that she yet again is keeping things from me, not fully trusting either of us. I'm not sure why it hurts as much as it does, but the feeling of betrayal stabs at my stomach. Part of me feels defeated, wanting to hear more about DD's beliefs, but the feeling of betrayal overrides everything else.

I force myself to stay quiet as I exit the cathedral, not caring about the service anymore. It's not like I'm disturbing anyone since no one can see me. I pass right through the crowd of people, none of them reacting to my presence as expected.

I feel Travis right on my tail. He's probably feeling worse about this revelation than I am, seeing as they've been together in this makeshift family for at least three times as long as I have.

"All this talk about staying away from other Wanderers and from places we are drawn to. What a joke," Travis scoffs, tugging on his suit jacket, adjusting it as he shakes his head back and forth in disbelief. "You know, I actually thought she was telling the truth about the draw and its consequences, but here she is breaking all of her own rules! But no, no, no; we have to follow them because we can't handle it."

"You think she's drawn here because of her waking life?"

"You saw the look on her face! All of them had it. Like they just took a tab," he snaps, pacing around the entryway to the castle-like building behind us. "For fuck's sake!" he yells throwing his arms up in the air and resting them on his forehead as he faces up toward the sky.

I look back at the cathedral's daunting double doors, realizing that it must be the same for DD as it is for me and the dance studio. I can't believe I felt bad about going to the studio and for not telling her about it when she's been hiding this the whole time.

"Fuck it. I need to take a walk," Travis says, not bothering to wait for me, leaving me alone in front of the church. I stand there awkwardly rubbing my arms, fighting against the sudden chill around me, not knowing what to do with myself. A chorus of rhythmic chanting comes from the congregation within the cathedral, echoing out to me, as if punching me in the gut again. I can't help but want to scream at them for not seeing me, for praising a god that left me behind. If he's even real at all.

"Can I ask you a question?" I ask, my voice dipping lower, letting Marvel know that I'm serious.

He turns his attention away from the dancers to face me, cocking an eyebrow, signaling me to continue instead of verbally responding.

"Why do you come to this specific dance studio if you aren't drawn to it? I mean, you're not getting a high from it like I am, but you come here anyway."

He leans back, looking at the ceiling fan in the center of the studio, pondering my question for a moment. The two of us have been coming here for some time now, and I couldn't help but ask, wondering if he's not drawn to it the same way I am.

"I guess this is where I last saw my wife before she moved on," he answers, still staring up at the ceiling, a blank expression on his face.

"You saw someone from your waking life?" I ask, all but shouting across the studio, staring at him in amazement. A million questions swarm my brain, but he speaks up before I have the chance to start verbalizing any of them.

"Yeah," he chuckles solemnly, his usually cheerful face morphing into a distant gaze that makes me want to cry for him. "The moment she materialized before me in the hospital I knew who she was to me. It wasn't a complete recognition, but I could feel it in my gut." He smiles, looking up as Emma and Florence start their mirrored chaine turn sequence around Vaughn in the center of the room. "She was beautiful," he continues, not breaking his eyes away from the girls. "She looked up at me and I knew she was special. It took everything in me to walk away, knowing that if I spoke to her, I wouldn't be able to resist the pull toward her and sink into madness."

"So, you just walked away? But I thought you said you last saw her here? Didn't you meet her at the hospital?"

"I was drawn to a hospital without realizing it at the time, which is where I saw her die and appear before me in her white gown. It took everything within me to not speak with her, but I did follow her," he says, pausing to take a deep breath before continuing. "I'm not sure if she ever realized she was dead. She spent the next few days wandering around the town like the others just passing through."

"Travis calls people like that Freshies and says we should just leave them be because they are less likely to freak out or harm themselves if they don't know the truth," I say, wondering if that's why he didn't say anything to her. Does he have the same experiences as DD and Travis with obnoxious Wanderers or confused Freshies?

"That, and the fact that it could lead to either of us becoming a Shell," he says grimly, scratching at his head again.

A Shell. That's what Travis mentioned before when we ran into that creature. I guess their origins are really old wanderers like DD told him, and not just something she said to scare us.

"I couldn't risk her becoming one of those mindless monsters, let alone be the reason she would have to deal with her own death and mourn both of us before moving on. This life is a pain I wouldn't wish upon my worst enemy. I didn't want that for her," he pauses again, letting out a choked, breathy sigh before continuing. "She was drawn here, spending the entirety of her last day here before she disappeared just outside this studio."

We both fall silent, watching as Avery and Sybil replace Emma and Florence around Vaughn, repeating the same mirrored turn sequence. Vaughn dances in the center of the room, almost in a circle, avoiding the girls like he did before, the only difference being that his attention is caught by Sybil at the end of the sequence as she takes the spotlight with her flawless fouettés.

"I think this place was special to her in her walking life,

despite not being drawn here myself," Marvel says, breaking our silence as the music picks up, Vaughn and Sybil starting their duet. "I like to think she used to dance here as a child. Maybe she was like them, dedicating herself to the art of ballet?"

I try to imagine Marvel as a young man standing outside the ballet studio, just walking by to meet up with his friends at the diner down the street, stopping instantly as he catches a glimpse of his wife in the window. He's mesmerized, mouth agape with the same gleam in his eyes he had as he watched Noah the other day. I wonder if he marveled at her beauty like that? Every day, he'd encourage her as she worked hard during practice just like the kids do. The love in his eyes despite not having any memories of her, love just functioning on a feeling, makes it obvious. The image of the two of them together is so tangibly sweet, and I can't imagine him being any other way.

"I also met you here." he chuckles, playfully nudging my knee, almost knocking me over in the process, bringing me back to reality. "And now I have someone to appreciate the art with me."

I see the tears swelling in his eyes and decide to let any further questions go, not wanting to see him cry or face those feelings any more than he already has.

Chapter 6

Red

I lean back on my elbows, sticking my feet out, as Travis goes on about some famous baseball player he saw in town. I absentmindedly run my fingers through the tall blades of grass beside me, not bothering to feign fascination as I tune out of the conversation. I've felt better since I told Travis and DD about Marvel, even though they don't realize that I've gone back to see him again. I still haven't told them about the dance studio, and I'm not sure if I ever will, despite how guilty I feel about going there and keeping secrets from them.

"Ughh! He was so hot!" Travis all but yells, pulling my attention back to him as he huffs dramatically next to me. "DD, you're just a prude. Riv, I know you would've thought he was just gorg too. Maybe you could go with me next time and we can ogle some hot guys at the club? I heard about this new one downtown that's supposed to be super fun."

"Why go if you can't even talk to anyone?" DD says, waving her hand as if dismissing the idea. "Even if you did run into another Wanderer, they are usually obnoxious.

Besides, you can't even have a normal conversation over all the loud music."

"I've never been to a club," I say, trying to prevent an argument and change the subject, although I'm not really sure if I want to go into town again. I'm not completely closed off to the idea, but all the strange feelings I got last time I went into town made me feel anxious. "I mean, it's not like I'd remember if I had or not," I add realizing they would've already known about most of my experiences post death.

"I think in February sometime. I'll have to look into it," she says, brushing the nonexistent dust off her dress as she walks down one of the moldy bait isles. "I've been thinking about Travis suggesting we go to that night club, and I think we should go out and do more things like that. I'm not saying we should go to the city too frequently, but maybe every once in a while. If we are all together, it'd be fine."

I want to snap at her. How can she be such a hypocrite? Maybe she's trying to make amends in her own way, sensing something is wrong without having a full-out confrontation. I wouldn't put it past her to pick up on the hostility and not make any attempt to address it. It's like she has a sixth sense for that sort of thing but also refuses to take responsibility for her own mistakes. Thankfully, Travis is still away, otherwise that might have started a whole fight between them that they would drag me into.

"Are we still going to the club tonight?" I ask, trying to change the topic away from the ballet. Two can play the guilt avoidance game.

"I'd assume so," she says, surprisingly seeming excited about the trip into town. "I don't think Travis would want to miss this."

"Miss what?" Travis asks, sounding completely monotone. Startled from his sudden appearance, we both look over to the doorway where Travis now stands. He stands awkwardly still, the skin around his eyes looking leathery and darker than usual. His hair stands up in odd directions as if he had been consistently running his hands through it since I last saw him, and his typically fresh-pressed pants are wrinkled with dirt lingering on his knees.

"What on earth happened to you?" DD questions before I can, rushing over to him.

He shrugs, only frowning in response as DD ushers him to lean over so she can fix his messy hair. She quickly rakes her fingers through it so that it lays flat again not noticing or choosing to ignore the tension in the air.

"There you go," she says cheerfully. "We were just talking about going to the club tonight like you suggested. Do you still want to go?"

"Sure," he says, calmly walking past her. "I've got the perfect place in mind."

"Perfect! We should probably head out, so we get into the city on time," DD says, clapping her hands as she turns to walk through the door.

I stare at Travis expectantly, finally catching his gaze. He just smirks down at me, not helping the anxious knot forming in my stomach. Travis can sometimes be a hothead, lashing out and picking fights with DD for fun, but that's about as far as it goes. I've been expecting a big argument between him and DD whenever he got back, but not the complete calm he's exhibiting now. They are both acting strange and it's starting to freak me out.

Travis follows DD out the door first and I quickly run out after them. As annoyed with DD as I am at the moment, I can't help but feel like this might be a time when I'll have to intervene when they finally do blow up at each other.

Something about their attitudes just seem too perky and calm.

We walk for what feels like days' worth of DD pestering Travis with a million questions about where we are going and how he found this place. She hasn't completely abandoned her motherly, hovering attitude. It's Travis's demeanor that worries me the most as we travel further and further away from the tackle shack. He just answers her questions without cracking a joke or protesting. I don't miss their bickering, but this feels unnatural. It's almost as if he's being... polite.

I find myself eventually walking a few steps behind them, my mind wandering away from the current moment. I try to think of anything in my past interactions with them where they acted like this, or even any situation that has caused sudden shifts in their personalities. There was one time that Travis convinced DD that I wasn't going to stay with them anymore, causing her to get quieter and more standoffish than usual, but Travis still poked fun at her while he was pulling the con. He didn't let me in on that prank until afterwards, but there also wasn't a real reason or angry motive behind it. Usually, they just yell at each other and quickly makeup when they piss each other off. Something about this doesn't just seem like another one of his 'long cons' as he likes to call them either.

Crowds of the living swarm the strip, loud music blasting from each of the bars. I try my best to keep up with Travis and DD, attempting to figure out what's going on with them. Both are acting strange, and I don't think they've had it out or anything yet. Maybe this isn't a good idea. Maybe we should just follow DD's usual paranoia and go back to the tackle shop.

Travis moves to walk ahead of us toward a building with

a singular door and a bouncer who is preventing a line of people from entering. Walking closer to the building, I feel my stomach tighten, hearing the bass of the music without having to be inside. We sidestep the line of people, walking right past the bouncer before stepping through the plum-colored door.

The uneasy feeling I had a moment ago disappears the second we step into the club. The vibration of the music seems to pass through me and everyone else in the room, lights flashing to the rhythmic beat, reflecting off sweaty bodies. The scent of cigarettes and body odor take over my senses as a group of drunk boys pass through me on their way to the dance floor, where a hoard of young adults dance, mostly offbeat, to the music. It's not the smell or the lights that put me at ease, but something else I can't quite identify.

Travis doesn't hesitate to push past the rows of people waiting by the bar, walking straight up to the cute guy at the front. He props his elbow up as if he were leaning against the countertop in an alluring way. I hesitantly follow him further into the bar with an overstimulated DD close behind. I try not to laugh as he looks up at the other man, a sultry smile sneaking across his face, mouthing something inaudible in his ear.

The cute guy jolts to the side, moving right through Travis revealing a couple seated beside him. They bump into the man again, making him scoff, stand and pick up his beer. They don't bother to apologize or even look his way as they remain eyes closed, and lips locked. Travis groans as the man walks away from the bar as if he had any chance of getting lucky. Turning toward DD, it becomes clear that Travis is way more comfortable in this environment than DD is, the uneasy expression on her face telling me all I need to know about her regrets on the decision to come here.

"Let's go dance," I yell to DD over the loud music, not bothering to wait for her protests before pulling her arm and dragging her out onto the dance floor.

For once, my invisibility feels normal, like I'm one with the crowd. I pull DD through toward the back and decide to park right next to a group of girls, mostly dressed in different shades of pink. One of the girls starts grinding, in what seems like it's intended to be a sexy way, on another girl in white with a 'bride-to-be' sash slung across her shoulder. The bride-to-be yells excitedly and throws her hands in the air, effectively splashing her fruity drink all over the scruffy looking man behind her. The disgruntled man storming off seems to help DD loosen up, and she and I both laugh after him. I'm suddenly glad that can't happen to us since nothing can touch us. I never thought I'd be grateful that I can't touch anything, but death keeps surprising me.

I try to match my movements to the people around me, making my boney shoulders move in a circular motion despite knowing that I probably look like a velociraptor on roller skates. I figured that since I'm pretty sure I used to be a dancer, I'd at least be a decent dancer here as well. That doesn't seem to be the case. DD either doesn't notice or care, dancing to her own beat, blonde curls flying around as she swings her head side to side. She throws her fisted hands in the air, pumping them up and down a second behind the base, smiling up at me from between sweaty bodies. Any onlooker would think this scene looks bizarre: a six-year-old, dressed almost like a child's doll, partying in a night club around a bunch of drunken adults dancing provocatively. It's almost comical, knowing she's pretty much a grumpy old lady inside.

I throw my head back and laugh, not sure why I was so worried earlier. I let myself enjoy the music as Travis joins us on the dance floor. The three of us are such an odd trio. I can't help wondering if we would've met and been friends if we all lived during the same time. Probably not. It's one of the things about the Blue I'm grateful for.

I let myself have fun for the first time in a while. I pretend the three of us are alive, becoming one with the crowd. We belong here.

"You wanna see something more entertaining," Travis asks, yelling in my ear so I can hear while also putting me at risk for bursting an eardrum. He pulls away, smirking mischievously at me, spiking my curiosity.

I nod my head, holding my hand over my ear while smiling back, knowing whatever he's going to show me is going to be interesting for sure. He tugs my hand, yelling at DD, telling her we'll be right back.

"Where are we going?" I yell over the music as he pulls me toward a door that has white letters spelling 'bathroom' on the outside.

Travis just laughs, yanking me into the bathroom through the black door. The whole room is lit up with neon purple signs, and my eyes are instantly pulled to a couple from the bar sucking each other's faces.

"They were at the bar earlier getting pretty handsy, and I saw them walking toward the bathroom while we were dancing," he says, snickering like a little kid about to cause mild mischief for their parents.

I laugh at their drunken sloppiness and shake my head at Travis for bringing me in here. "So predictable." I look up at the couple, grinding against each other like desperate, wild hyenas, breathing heavily against each other's wet lips.

"Oh, what'd I'd do to be able to get laid. They don't know how lucky they are." Travis groans dramatically, pouting and gesturing toward them. "Well, that's enough of a show for me. We should leave before this heats up too much."

Travis moves to leave the bathroom and I go to follow him, but I suddenly can't seem to move my feet. My stomach clenches and I open my mouth to say something, but nothing comes out. I try to breathe in, but I can't get any air into my lungs, my mind focusing on suppressing the sudden bile that's rising in my throat. The jingling of pants interrupts the sound of lips smacking and the woman curses as she awkwardly struggles to unclasp the snaps of her body suit.

You, disgusting whore.

"You coming?" Travis asks, no longer focused on the couple or trying to leave, but I can't rip my eyes away, only hearing that voice again. "I don't know about you, but I'm not really into voyeurism," Travis jokes, but I can't laugh.

It's all your fault. You were asking for it.

"River, what's wrong?" Travis gently touches my arm and I instinctively flinch away, my skin burning where his fingertips touched.

You want this. Scream. Scream in pleasure, you slut. You like the pain. Don't you?

The man's hand grabs the woman's ass, and I feel familiar thick, grimy hands touch my stomach just under the hem of my shirt and over the jeans of my left thigh. I instantly slap them away, only to see that there's no one touching me. No one's there. The same grimy hands slide up my shirt, pushing my bra to the side. They press against my breasts, squeezing them before pinning me against the wall. I can't move. I can't breathe.

Disgust for myself consumes me as the hand on my thigh moves upwards. I try to force my way out, but the hands hold me in place. I can't escape. I want to disappear again. I want to be invisible once more. I want to die. I want to really die. I don't want to exist or have to feel anything anymore.

You should die.

The metal door to the first bathroom stall slams shut, closing us off from the couple, although we can still hear their pants. I crouch down, somehow feeling the coolness of the tiles beneath me and behind me, rubbing against my skin. I try to imagine the woman digging her nails into the man's bicep, moaning in pleasure as he thrusts into her, but all I hear are screams. My screams. An echoing of "no" and "stop" play in a loop, getting louder and louder.

The lights in the room become deeper and more vivid, turning bright red as everything around me blurs as if a bomb just went off and affected my vision. I can't see Travis anymore. It's just me, the metal door, and the ghost hands touching my body.

Your body's reaction shows how much you want it. It's all your fault. Whore. Slut. Used piece of trash. No one will want you now.

"River," I hear DD yell, grabbing my face in her hands, pulling me toward her, blocking my view of the door. Her blue eyes look right into mine, a sense of calm coming over me as I remember where I am. The feeling of hands touching me fades away and I try to force myself to look at Travis again.

How did she get here? When did she get here?

Travis stands awkwardly to the side, twisting his ring

77

around, not sure what to do with his hands, looking down at me with an expression of sympathy that makes me feel worse than I already do. DD wipes my cheeks with the pads of her thumbs, and I realize I was crying.

"Let's go home," she says gently, helping me up to my feet.

Run away like a coward. You can't escape yourself. You can't escape the truth.

We walk past the crowd of people drinking and dancing, but the sense of belonging I felt earlier is no longer there. It feels like everyone is staring at me, despite no one being able to see me. They don't even know I exist. Do I really exist, though? I'm dead. What would you even call this?

DD doesn't let go of my hand, pulling me out of the bar the same way I pulled her into the crowd moments ago, while Travis just follows close behind. I can't bring myself to look at either of them. We walk the rest of the way to the tackle shop in silence. I'm glad, though, because I still can't seem to form words. I'm not sure what happened, but all I feel like doing right now is somehow becoming more invisible than I already am.

Go die, filthy bitch.

Chapter 7

Purple

I f I didn't see it, I wouldn't have noticed the baby cockroach crawling through my arm, making its way toward an empty filing cabinets along the back wall. It must think it's alone in here, with only the light from a crack under the door to make the room visible.

My whole body feels numb. My limbs are raw from my attempts at scratching the feeling away. The feeling of terror... of those hands on my body. Part of me is glad I can't sleep, as my dreams would only be filled with nightmares, as if I'm not already reliving the scene in my head over and over.

I count the ceiling tiles again, now used to the dim lighting in the room. Twenty-four, again.

It's been quiet, besides DD checking in on me every few days, or what I think are a few days. In her mind, it's probably better that I work out this problem in isolation rather than going back to the club to find out more about what triggered me. Surprisingly, I haven't seen Travis since we left the club. He's the first person I thought would be here for me if something like this were to happen. He was so protective of me back when we saw that monster and was there to support me at the church. I thought he'd be here for me when I started turning into one of those monsters.

I count the ceiling tiles again. Twenty-four.

I don't remember getting back to tackle shack. Only DD's blue eyes bringing me back to reality then these damn ceiling tiles.

The cockroach finally makes it to the metal filing cabinets and somehow squeezes into the one on the bottom, left most drawer. It's not the first one I've seen crawl in there since I've been in this dark room. There must be a family of them living here with us, although they aren't aware of our presence among them. They are just like me.

Such disgusting creatures.

DD would tell me not to think about what happened at the club, but I can't help it. The feeling of wanting to completely disappear didn't seem to come from just nowhere. I can't seem to get my mind off it, wondering if it has something to do with my death.

Since being in the Blue, I've been so confused as to what happened to me, and as to why I would be stuck here. Doesn't anyone care about me in the waking world? Am I really that insignificant that no one cared to put my body to rest? Did I do this to myself? Was I really some terrible person that isolated myself so much so that no one noticed that I was gone? Do I really mean nothing?

You're isolating yourself now. Why would anyone care about you?

DD yells echo through the walls toward the main floor of the tackle shop. Travis must have come back. Why else would she raise her voice? Travis laughs then starts yelling back at her. This is probably going to turn into a whole fight since he's been gone for so long. I can't bring myself to go out and stop them. I can't handle this. I'm not sure how long he's been gone this time, but it's weird for even him to have disappeared for longer than a week. It's been more than that, I think. The longer I'm in the Blue the less able I am to keep up with the ongoings of the waking world.

I finally get up and decide to leave the tackle shop again, not wanting to listen to them argue anymore. I'm hoping a change of scenery might help me to get over this funk I'm in. I walk through the back wall and hope their yelling keeps them distracted long enough for me to make my escape.

I walk down the dirt road toward the dance studio, wanting to feel the high that comes when I'm there without the uncomfortable feelings like at the club. The familiar cursive letters of 'Tonya's Dance' glowing purple remind me of the lights in the club and I unconsciously flinch at the memory. I push past the headache forming in my mind, walking through the glass. The familiar buzz of electricity spikes up my arms, igniting a relaxing sense of security I've been lacking for a while now.

The big, blue world around me seems to be ever-changing, and I've come to take a small pleasure in being alone. Now, don't get me wrong, I still wish I could be a part of it all, and I can't help but wonder why I'm here. I watch as the students shuffle into the first studio for practice, lining up on either side of the open barre. I look at my thin form in the mirror on the side wall: my elongated, bony arms making it seem as though I'd fit in amongst the others standing in first position in their black leotards. Assuming I look the same age that I died at, I couldn't be more than seventeen years old. What happened to me? I've been a Wanderer long enough now to know that I'm not going anywhere. My body isn't being put to rest. I'm stuck here, just watching, for apparently all of eternity.

I notice Avery isn't in attendance today and I get a strange and probably terrible idea. I look around the studio halls to see if Marvel, or worse, DD, are lurking, just waiting to catch me doing something stupid, but they are nowhere to be found. I feel the familiar tug inside, telling me to join them.

Dance with them.

I walk further into the room, falling in line right between a much taller Noah and Harrison, pretending to place my hand around the open space on the barre. Classical music pierces the air and a rhythmic buzz sparks inside me; I'm aflame with a high I've never felt before. I quickly tendu in front of me, following in step with the rest of the class, as if on instinct. I tell myself that I only know the steps since I've been watching them learn these drills since they were merely toddlers, but I know this feeling of familiarity and instinct isn't something that someone can just pick up from observing. It comes from years and years of intense training. I ignore DD's warnings and the thoughts from the club lingering in the back of my head and let the addictive rush turn my world more purple and delicious. This time, however, the purple hue that replaces the blue isn't as painful. It's pure bliss.

Dance. You love it. You belong here.

Since Avery is gone, I take her place as Noah's dance partner for the rest of the day, knowing he can't really lift me during across the floor warmups, but I don't care. I let myself imagine him lifting me high as I leap gracefully beside him, watching a grown Sybil and Vaughn in the mirror as if they were us. They look so graceful, almost adults now. It seems as if just yesterday I was laughing as Emma, Avery, and Sybil argued over whether bubble gum or chocolate chip cookie dough was the better ice cream flavor. Their chubby fingers were all sticky, covered in a mix of flavors from the parlor next door, when Sybil and Emma declared that bubble gum was better because it was pink. Now, they're in a new stage of life. And I'm... still here. My feet stop moving and Noah passes completely through me to the other end of the studio. The high I was once feeling dissipates. I step away before Harrison and Florence have the chance to pass through me as well, not wanting to be reminded even more of my frozen finitude.

I look into the mirror: my eyes look glazed over and are more of a deep purple, almost red. I let out a small scream, not sure what's happening. The music cuts out and the entire room is instantly dark. Everyone yelps or freezes for a moment. Then it hits me. I did that.

Yes. You did.

"I'll go check the breaker," the instructor says, leaving the room. "You guys stay here and stretch or get some water until I get back."

Holy crap. That was me! But what does this mean?

You belong here. Keep dancing. Ignore it. You love the feeling, so ignore what's happening. Dance.

I look at myself in the mirror again, slightly horrified. Looking closer at my face, I can't avoid the crazed look in my bloodshot eyes, appearing as if they are trying to tear out of my skull. I almost don't recognize myself. It's then that I realize this is what DD and Travis warned me about. The only difference from Travis's explanation is that I still have my wits about me.

Besides looking a bit scary and getting a high-like feeling, I'm not sure what DD was so afraid of. However, in all her warnings she failed to mention the fact that you could interfere with the waking world. That's seems like a major thing to leave out.

Maybe she doesn't know. Maybe if she knew then she wouldn't be so against learning about our pasts. Maybe we were wrong this whole time! What if we should be looking into our pasts and that is what will allow us to move on?

I turn to run back to the tackle shack, excited to tell Travis and DD about my discovery and new theory. This could change everything!

Don't leave! You want this.

I unwillingly freeze. I look down at my feet, trying to take another step forward, but they won't budge. Fear creeps up my spine and I collapse to the ground.

Don't go. Keep dancing. Don't you want to dance?

It's just like the bathroom at the club.

I try to force the fear down, focusing on DD and Travis. We might be able to change how we live. We just need to figure out how to control our emotions. We can do that. I can do this.

I crawl away from the kids, getting closer to the glass wall. I need to get out of here. I need to get back to my family. I push myself harder, ignoring the voice inside my head, screaming at me to stay. Closer. Closer.

I don't bother to look around for Marvel or DD, not caring if either of them see me as I crawl back through the glass studio walls and onto the cemented sidewalk. I ignore the familiar feeling pulling me back toward the studio and run all the way back to the tackle shack, knowing I need to get back to the tackle shack and talk to DD and Travis about this potentially death-changing discovery.

· · ·

"What do you mean you've been meeting up with him for weeks?" DD yells, her voice carrying into the backroom as I walk back through the wall. "Travis, that's crazy. You know what's gonna happen to you!"

I go to the main floor, hoping my discovery will get them to stop arguing about whatever they are upset about this time. I am stopped in my tracks by Travis slamming his fist into the wall, making it shake. The action causes some of the chipped paint pieces to fall off completely and my whole body tenses.

"I told you, my name is actually Steven," he snaps back, glaring at DD with bright red, crazed eyes. Gasps escape both of our mouths, shocked by his action. Not just because of his anger, but also because his hand contacted the wall at all. It's happening to him too, but there is a slight difference in the way he looks compared to how I looked in the studio. His eyes aren't just glowing red, but they look hungry and panicked, a certain desperation behind his gaze that screams danger.

My stomach knots and I feel frozen in place again.

DD looks over to me, just now realizing that I'm also in the room, her thin lips souring as she contemplates what to do. I meet her gaze and see the terror in her eyes as she silently begs me for help.

"I don't understand what's so bad about welcoming a new person into our lives," Travis says, manically twisting his ring around his finger. "He's one of us now, so why? Why can't you just let me be happy?"

I open my mouth to ask what's going on, but an unfamiliar, deep voice beats me to it. "Steven? What's going on?" A frail, old man comes around the corner peering into the tackle shop curiously. "Is this your family?" he asks, taking note of DD and I inside. Travis physically relaxes, moving to open the door for the elderly man to walk through. "Thank you, hun," he says, smiling lovingly up at Travis.

Travis smiles back at him, the anger from a second ago disappearing. The crazed look in his eyes is more than just his usual mischief. Something is off about him.

"Oh, well, aren't you just two beautiful young ladies," the old man says, waving a swollen hand to greet us. I instantly notice the familiar gold ring on his pinky finger. It's easy to identify as a matching set, as it's identical to Travis's. Then it clicks in my mind. They knew each other from their waking lives.

"I'm River," I say, introducing myself, my voice quivering a bit more than I intended it to. I nervously glace at DD, who stands completely still with her mouth agape. I extend my hand for him to shake when Travis growls at me, effectively stopping me from taking his hand. My gaze snaps to Travis's, seeing his eyes glowing an even brighter red, shifting between DD and I, as if not able to fully recognize us, before settling on his lover once again. "Ummm DD?"

"Travis," DD says, her voice shaking, taking notice of his strange behavior and seeming to understand what's happening to him more than I do. "You need to calm down. We are your friends, your Wanderer family. Remember us? It's River and DD."

He growls again, sounding more and more like an animal. Dark red, almost black clouds circle his body, bleeding out from the orifices within him. A familiar cold rushes over me and I instinctly take a step backwards. The smoke swarms around him like a poisonous gas images of a younger version of the man in front of us flashing through the cloud like scenes from a film. DD tries to reach for him, but I pull her back. Her wild eyes snapping at me, pleading with me to let her run to him, but I only tighten my grip not knowing what might happen to her if she gets any closer to Travis.

The old man looks around as if he is just noticing the smoke around him, concern lacing his features as he's starting to realize that something is amiss with his lover. The poor man is probably feeling even more confused, as his memories from his previous life must be slipping away, making this scene before him even more mind boggling. Images of a fit young man, his hair just starting to thin at the back, but not yet near the point where it is now steps into view, panic lacing his eyes. The old man's younger self sobs as a group of laughing twenty-somethings pull him backwards.

The image in the smoke cuts to another man with a long face, but the same crooked nose as the old man. He grins and my body skin turns cold. Burning bile creeps up my throat as the gravity seems to grow stronger around us. It's not bile. It's a familiar feeling.

DD tries to pull back her arm, scolding me, but I don't loosen my grip. I tune her sound out. The man's face is blurred, the smoke turning an even deeper shade of burgundy.

"I'm so sorry, Steven," the old man says, gently caressing Travis's face, as if he didn't notice the chaos that is over-taking him. "I tried to stop them from doing this to you. It's all my fault. If only I never told my brother about you, they never would've come for us."

Travis scratches at his arms and I fully take in his appearance. His normally well-fitting suit seems to be swimming on him. The material is practically falling off his shoulders, almost appearing tattered and tearing at the seams. His face is sunken in, and his teeth appear as though they are turning a dark gray color, making him look like some sort of junkie. What happened to him? It looks like he's been starved and beaten, and now this?

He moves toward DD and me. Both of us take a few steps back as he pushes over a display of fishing lures at the front of the store. A small yelp escapes my lips, as I'm still shocked by his ability to touch things in the waking world.

"What's wrong, hun?" the elderly man asks, pressing his wrinkled hand to Travis's cheek, bringing his attention back to him. I expect to see the same loving glance as before, but instead Travis only holds an expression of lustful hunger that can be associated with rage. The expression somehow seems so familiar, despite looking so odd associated with Travis's face. My body involuntarily quivers at the sight. The redness from his eyes start to bleed into the crevices of his skin, pouring from his mouth, nose, and eyes in almost veinlike tendrils.

"River, we need to get out of here now," DD states under her breath, her face switching back and forth between utter terror and protective-mom mode. The fear in her eyes makes my stomach tighten, justifying my suspicions about Travis.

Before either of us has the chance to react, Travis's jaw drops unnaturally, morphing to extend halfway down his body. His almost black-coated teeth extend and sharpen into points. The old man doesn't have time to register what's happening before Travis's mouth chomps down around the top half of his body. Dark blue, thick liquid shoots in every direction as Travis's teeth tear into the man's flesh, coating both DD and me. The bottom half of the elderly man slumps onto the ground: his knees slamming into the floor first, followed by his lower torso. His severed left hand smacks against the blood-soaked cement near where his intestines have spilled out, rolling onto the floor, one end still hanging from Travis's contorted jaws.

I grab DD's hand and turn toward the nearest wall, facing away from Travis and the smoke around him. I'm not hesitating to do as she says, but I won't risk leaving her behind. The air around us starts to feel heavy, as if the earth's gravity has suddenly multiplied by ten. My legs wobble, struggling to move, as I pull DD and I past the rows of merchandise and through the nearest wall.

We sprint as fast as we can up the hill, our adrenaline spiking an all-time high. Everything feels as though time has slowed down as Travis lets out a high-pitched scream. The sound ripples through my body with a force so powerful it knocks both DD and I onto the grassy hill. I stare down at the grass as my face smashes into the dirt, and for a second the grass looks greener, and the dirt is brown. I blink a few times as my vision starts to spot and flash between what seems to be the colors of the waking world and the Blue. I glance beside me, and for a quick moment I am able to see the true pastel blush of DD's dress, and I gasp. Time stands still as the world practically warps around us and the tingling, euphoric sensation I usually get at the dance studio passes through me.

It doesn't last for more than a moment, though, my vision dulling back to the blue hue I've grown accustomed to, and I remember where we are and why. The terror I felt in the tackle shack returns. DD looks back at me, seeming to have her wits about her, which is more than I can say about myself I feel like I'm having an emotional whiplash. She seems to notice my struggle, reaching out a hand as I attempt to push myself up off the ground.

Neither of us attempt to look back at the tackle shop, too scared of what might be back there. DD tightens her grip on my hand, tugging me back up to my feet, her mommode kicking in full gear again. Then, we run.

Chapter 8

Calm

We run until we get to the edge of the city and night takes over the sky. We both plop down on the cement, not caring that both people and cars are passing through us. My feet ache and my stomach feels sick.

I'm not sure what inner sense of self-preservation kicked in, telling me to get away from Travis as fast as I could before he imploded. If that's even what happened. I'm not sure if he is dead-dead, alive-dead, or able to snap out of it somehow.

"What just happened?" I ask, sitting up to glare at DD, not leaving any room for her to dodge my questions anymore.

DD stares up at the stars, not saying anything, and I snap.

"What on earth are you doing?" I yell, throwing my hands in the air. "I have done nothing but trust you and listen to you this whole time, and now our friend implodes, and you have nothing to say?"

She turns on her side, facing away from me, still silent.

"Oh my... for fuck's sake!" I yell, releasing a scream into the sky as if it'll somehow make me feel better. "I know you've been lying to Travis and me about the church, which probably has something to do with Travis acting so strange lately and going on a rampage. And I never said anything! I just kept holding my tongue, hoping you'd one day open up to me and tell me the truth about all your Wanderer buddies at the church and how you've been drawn there this whole time. But, no. You won't even tell me about what's happening to Travis." I huff, laying back down on the street with my legs sprawled out.

"He's a Shell," she says between sniffles, her voice cracking as she says it.

I stiffen for a moment, partially in shock because I've never seen her cry before. Her little body shakes as she tries to contain herself, and I feel myself soften.

"Hey, it's okay, DD. I'm sorry for yelling at you. I should've said something earlier about the church thing. It's unfair for me to lash out at you all at once."

"No," she sobs, turning to face me completely, tears pouring down her round face. "You're right. It's all my fault. I should've told you all the truth from the beginning. Travis wouldn't have become a Shell if he knew the truth."

I'm taken aback for a second, trying to connect the dots that don't seem to have any link. "But Travis knew about the Shells. He told me about them."

"No," she interrupts, sobbing harder, rubbing at her eyes. "It is my fault. I didn't tell him everything. I didn't want to face the truth of what happened all those years ago, so I wouldn't talk about it, and now he's gone too."

"Gone?" I question, pulling her hands away from her face to check and make sure I understood her right. What does she mean 'gone?' Did he move on or explode into nothingness? Can we get him back?

"You saw his eyes," she says, repetitively sniffing and wiping her nose, trying to compose herself again. "The way he was talking and then that blast of energy. It's what happened last time too. There's no coming back from that."

"Back from what? What happened to Travis? And what do you mean by 'last time?'"

"He's a Shell, as in a shell of his former self. He's now doomed to walk around like an empty husk of a soul, terrorizing other ghosts for all eternity because he learned too much about his previous life. It's like a breach between worlds and our soul-bodies can't handle it," she says, pausing as she lets out a sob. "If I'm being honest, I don't think we were meant to be here. There's a reason every single group in every region throughout time has processes for putting bodies to rest. We accidentally found loopholes."

"Okay," I reply, dragging out the word. "We aren't supposed to be here. What does that have to do with Travis turning into a Shell?"

"I'm not exactly sure how it works, but I have a theory that since we aren't supposed to be stuck here, that when we connect too many dots between our world and the waking world our bodies can't handle it and it causes breaches between worlds. Since our bodies can't handle it, we lose our minds, and there's no coming back."

I stare at her in utter shock, processing what she's saying, and it all makes sense. The red, crazed eyes, the purple vision, the headaches, the bombarding of emotions, the stomach pains, the almost high-like feeling that one could easily become addicted to.

Travis.

She said he was gone. Does that mean he can't come back to us? That he's completely lost his mind? That he's turned into some sort of monster?

"How do you know this," I ask, not sure if I really want an answer.

"I should've told you the truth years ago," she says hiccupping. "This isn't the first time I've seen someone turn into a Shell. It was the man who found me, Fill. I tried to warn you both, but I just couldn't bring myself to tell you what happened to Fill. I couldn't-" she sobs, unable to finish her sentence.

"So, you knew this would be the result of looking into our pasts?"

The look on her face tells me my understanding is correct. I wrap my arms around her, letting her sob, knowing that she feels responsible for everything after all this time. She's been the one holding both Travis and I together for this long, so I try to be strong for her. A few stray tears betray me as I too lost a friend and family member in the Blue.

"I should have seen the signs. I saw them in you before and was able to bring you back before, and I should've seen it with Travis," she cries, clutching on to me like a child. The chilling feeling of the club bathroom floods my mind and the warmth DD brought back to me, calming me from my own state of terror. I didn't feel crazed or chaotic back then, but lonely and scared. Did I look like Travis back then? Is that how Travis feels now?

"We can't go back," she says between hiccups. "To the tackle shack. We need to find a new place."

"Don't worry about that now. We'll figure something out," I say, trying to reassure her, but I can't really think about anything. It all just feels numb.

The sound of the river rushing past me is louder than it usually is, fighting against the rain as it pelts against the gravel and into the river itself. The water levels are higher than usual, and I'm entranced by the harsh movement within, large white caps forming around the boulders that line the other side of the river. I'm not entranced in the same way I have been at the dance studio, but the rushing water seems to ignite a healthier calm inside me. It's not so different from that day.

This is where it all started. This is where I met DD which led me to Travis. I can't believe he's a Shell. I can't believe I was stupid enough to not notice the changes within him. I know DD is feeling a lot of the blame right now, but so do I. I noticed him acting strange since the time we followed DD to the cathedral. I should've said something. I should have helped him.

I was too focused on my own problems after the club. I knew something was wrong that night. I should've said something to DD. I shouldn't have holed myself up in the backroom for so long. I shouldn't have second guessed their warnings. I shouldn't have gone back to the dance studio. He was always there for me when I was struggling. Travis needed me and I wasn't there for him.

Those visions of Travis's last moments were horrible. It was like I couldn't move. DD said I was like that at the club. I wonder what visions she saw from my life. Were they as horrible as Travis's? How did I end up in this river?

I told DD that I needed some time alone before we went to find a new place to inhabit, since Travis's Shell took over the tackle shack. I somehow ended up here. I wanted to go back to the dance studio, but I thought better of it. I can't risk DD being alone in the Blue and I'm the only one she has left. That means I need to protect myself and reduce the amount of exposure to potential Shell triggering people or places.

I know what I saw in that mirror the last time I went there. My eyes were purple, not blue, but also not red like Travis's. I didn't get to look in the bathroom mirror at the club, but everything around me had started to turn red. The aura around me in the bathroom was so cold and painful like the times I had been near a Shell, which was so different from how I feel at the dance studio. Both times I was faced with ghosts of my past, but the effect was different. I can't help but want to learn more about the effects of the studio, but I can't risk leaving DD alone and becoming a Shell myself. Seeing Travis like that wasn't just terrifying and bleakly depressing. It was like my friend had been possessed by some sort of demon, no trace of the fun-loving, goofy man I have come to know and care for. I can't let DD go through that again.

If he was here right now, he'd probably be making some joke about my self-loathing, pity party and suggest we go into the city to people watch again. Then he'd start another fight with DD about her being a 'wet rag all the time, putting a damper on his fun.' A laugh slips through my lips, barely audible as the wind picks up and the river sloshes around even more.

"I should've known you'd be here," DD says from behind me.

"I must have been here for longer than I thought," I reply, turning to face her, sending her a small, closed-lipped smile. "Sorry if I worried you."

She walks down the hill, sitting down beside me. The

two of us fall into a comfortable silence for a moment, not needing to ruminate on why one of us may worry about the other for being a part for a long time.

"I went to the church this morning. I just thought I should tell you, since we've decided to be more honest with each other," she says timidly, as if I would chastise her. Part of me wants to, but I also can't get mad when she's trying to be honest with me like I asked.

"Is that a good idea? Going back to that place, knowing it's a part of your old life, might not be the best idea," I reply, thinking about my own decision to stay away from the dance studio or to risk going back.

"I wanted to go back one last time to get some closure on some things." she sighs, wrapping her thin arms around her legs, pulling her knees to her chest. "I also wanted to pray for Travis there, hoping that God'll find some way to get that mess of a man up to heaven soon."

"How does that work? Praying?" I ask, hoping not to offend her by a potentially stupid question.

"You know, I'm not really sure how else to explain it, other than you just talk to God," she says, letting out a slight chuckle as she looks up at the sky in wonder. "You can tell him about anything: concerns, hopes, dreams, ask questions. It's really quite incredible."

"But how do you know he's listening or that he heard you?"

"You just feel it," she replies, smiling brightly. "It's like the whole world lights up and you feel warm, like you're being embraced."

I ponder on the idea for a moment, not really sure if I completely understand, but I also don't want to offend her by not feeling the same way. Instead, I try to change the subject.

"Did going back feel okay, though? Did you get what you needed?"

"I was actually going to suggest you do the same," she says, chewing on her bottom lip. "I was thinking we should move away from this area, since we'd be less likely to run into places or things that might cause us to become Shells."

I nod my head in response, feeling a bit sad that we'll truly have to leave everything behind, but also understanding her logic. Maybe I should go back to the studio one last time. I'd like to see the kids and say bye to Marvel. I guess one last time wouldn't hurt.

"Want to meet back here in three days, then we'll head out? Do you think that'll be enough time?"

"I'll be here," I reply, looking out at the rapids.

The road turns from gravel to pavement, and I feel the familiar pull. As I approach Tonya's Dance, I refrain from letting myself get sucked inside, standing just outside the glass by the bench. Avery and Emma walk by, talking about some celebrity drama they heard about online. I watch them as they pull on the black handle I've never been able to touch, opening the glass door. Their voices muffle as the door closes behind them.

Come in. Come dance.

For a second, I ponder over the idea to try and open the door. Maybe I'd be able to do it. Travis was able to move things because he became a Shell, and the power went out because of me last time I was here.

I reach my hand out, but I'm stopped by Marvel's voice.

"Don't do it." He sighs, almost sounding apathetic about it.

I let my hand fall to my side, too ashamed to look at him,

knowing he knows what I was trying to do. He knows about Shells, so he must know the steps to becoming one. There is no avoiding it.

"If you think you'd be able to turn that handle, then you've already seen the effects of what could happen when a Wanderer discovers things about their life among the living," he says sternly, sounding almost disappointed, which, for some reason, bothers me more than I thought it would.

"I know," I say, hanging my head like a scolded child. "I came to tell you that. I was only coming here hoping I'd run into you."

There's a pause. Neither of us falling into our usual casual banter. Neither of us wanting to say what needs to be said.

"I heard from the others about your friend," Marvel states matter-of-factly.

I ignore Marvel's comment, not wanting to discuss Travis yet. Instead, the two of us turn toward Avery and Noah, inaudibly arguing in Noah's silver Honda. I ponder over what Avery and Noah must be arguing about. I wonder if it is something of importance that will change the course of their lives or if it's one of their usual tiffs regarding something trivial that they'll both forget about by the end of the week. Either way, they'll forget about it by the time they become Wanderers. If they're lucky, they'll be put to rest and not have the chance to ponder such things. If only I could be so lucky.

I turn to face my friend, staring at the side of his round face, silently communicating to him what I can't seem to say out loud. He knows what will happen to me if I continue to come here, and why I have to leave.

Part of me wants to ask how he knew about Travis, but,

at the same time, I don't want to know. It appears I'm better off not knowing or asking too many questions about some things. All that matters is that he understands me and wants the best for me. That, I do know. I don't need to hear it from him to know that he cares.

"I should go," I say suddenly, not wanting to say goodbye to my friend, but also realizing that this is the last time we'll probably see each other in the Blue. No more dancing, no more kids. No more Marvel.

Neither of us say anything else, when suddenly I'm knocked to the ground by something hard. My whole body passes through the glass doors, my butt slamming onto the smooth cement flooring within the studio.

"What the hell, Noah," Avery snaps, pushing up against the small bench outside the studio to help her up off the ground. "Did you seriously just push me? Look. It's not my fault you got injured. You don't need to take me down with you."

She touched me. But how?

Marvel just stares blankly down at me, both of us not sure of what just happened. He hesitantly walks into the studio, glancing my whole body up and down warily, as if I am going to turn into a Shell at any moment.

Warmth fills my lungs and pulses through my body, the familiar tingling sensation coating my skin starting at the edge of my appendages. I look down to see my fingertips and toes appearing as though they were dipped in purple wax, fading from their typical shade of blue to indigo to almost lilac ombre. I don't bother to see Marvel's reaction, scurrying up off the floor and racing to the nearest mirror to see violet eyes staring back at me.

"Why am I still me? I'm not a Shell right? I'm still me," I call out to Marvel, not taking my eyes off my mirrored self. I trace the outline of my vibrant eyes with my purple fingers, a sense of calm taking over my senses.

"You're okay," Marvel states more as a question than a fact, inching closer to me.

"I'm okay," I say, a smile spreading across my face as I finally look back at my friend.

Chapter 9

Pierre

I practically run down the gravel road until it bleeds into unkempt grass, excited to tell DD about what's happening to me and my lack of turning into a Shell. Wait. I can't go back to the tackle shack. That's where Travis's Shell is. I can't be excited about this right now. We just lost Travis, and no matter how much I want to, we can't go back to the tackle shack. I never thought I'd miss the terrible scent of rotting fish and moldy paper, but I do. That place had become a sort of home for me, but I know that's not really what I miss. I wish I could talk to Travis. He'd know just the joke to get me feeling better again, and DD would go back to being her chipper, mom-like self, bickering at his dangerous behaviors.

His dangerous behaviors? They weren't too far off from my own. I don't know what I would do if I saw someone who recognized me on this side of the world. I'm not even sure of how he triggered him into turning into a Shell. I should have been there for him. Maybe I could have talked him down like DD did for me, when I was overcome with those terrible memories from my past. I can't imagine the overwhelming feelings he must have been dealing with the moment that man said his real name.

"Steven," I say out loud, just barely audible over the sound of rushing water getting louder as my feet absent-mindedly take me back to the river where I first met DD. The name sounds foreign on my lips, but somehow it makes sense for him. Steven, Travis, whatever his name is, he is my friend. He's a part of my family.

I can't blame him for letting his emotions from his waking life take over, instead I feel responsible. I should've seen the signs. He never felt like he was enough for DD and me, and I knew that. His desperation for the waking world, finding a purpose, consumed him, and I didn't do anything to help. All I could do was feel sorry for myself and question the same things. I still do.

I fall to my knees before the edge of the river and let myself cry. I cry not only for myself, but for my friend, who's no longer sane enough to recognize the people who care most about him. The man I knew is gone.

Sobs rack through my body before disappearing into the air where no one can hear them or see me. I don't know what to do anymore. I want to be there for DD, but I feel so lost.

Maybe Travis is happier now that he's a Shell? It doesn't seem like he has any control over himself, but at least he's not endlessly wondering anymore. What if that's better than this torturous life if you can even call this a life.

I don't know how long I end up sitting by the river, whether it's days or weeks that go by in the real world. I only lift my head when I hear a car door, slamming at the top of the hill.

Looking up, I see a young man cautiously walking toward the bridge, leaving behind a dingy, silver four-door vehicle behind him. I squint my eyes as if it'll help me to see clearly, hoping to identify the make and model of the vehicle or to see who's disturbing my peaceful pity party. Looking closer at the car, I notice there is a dent on the side of the driver's door, the body of the Honda seeming oddly familiar when it clicks.

It's Noah's car.

Noah's lanky frame slinks across the top of the hill, limping onto the small, metal bridge the city must have neglected over the years. He leans into one of the rusty beams. Despite being so far away and the rushing water preventing me from hearing him, I know he's crying. I'm not sure how, but like a sixth sense I know.

I all but jump off the grass, my bare feet pushing as hard as they can against the gravel, my skin prickling as I race toward the bridge.

Die.

As I get closer, I can see his boney frame contorting as he sobs, and I get this anxious feeling that something isn't right. I pump my legs harder, desperately trying to get to the top of the hill, the scene feeling familiar and terrifying at the same time.

Jump.

No, no, no. He can't be jumping. Don't do it! I run as fast as I can, screaming at him to stop, as if I could stop him.

Worthless. Slut. Nothing.

"Noah, stop! You can't," I yell, sprinting along the metal walkway. I reach out, trying to grab his arms and shake him back to reality. My fingers slip through his body repeatedly as I futilely try to push him away from the railing.

"It's pointless now," he says, as if responding to me like he's aware of my presence. He kicks out his leg, which I now realize is in a cast and a boot, hitting the railing, making it rattle. "It was all for nothing," he sobs into the air.

Jump. You're worthless anyway.

Fear courses through me and a sense of sadness pierces me, for more than just Noah. I feel the tears swell and fall down my cheeks as he hoists himself up on the handrails, the scene feeling so familiar as I fruitlessly try to pull him down. The feeling of overwhelming desolation consumes me, and I take a step back. It suddenly all makes sense. Why would anyone want to live when everything is just going to fall apart?

That's right. Worthless sluts like you should just die.

Yeah. There's no point in living when you just disappoint everyone.

No one's ever going to love you now. It's all your fault.

I'm a disgusting human and it'd be better if I just jumped.

I can't help but admire the ease in which he gracefully raises himself up above the bridge's edge. It's just like we were back in the studio, our roles reversed, and I'm holding him in the air. He's wonderful. He's talented. He has an entire future ahead of him.

Wait. He's got an entire future ahead of him. What was I thinking? He can't do this! He'll die if he jumps from this height.

I scream for help, but no one can hear me. I can't help him. No one is coming.

Die. Jump. Die!

I ignore the voice in my head, focusing only on Noah. He has so much to live for. I can't imagine why he'd want to kill himself.

I look down at his foot and realize it must be broken. A broken foot might have set him back in the dance world or even have ended his career, but who knows what other things he is good at or what he could learn to love about life. He might still be able to dance, but he won't be able to find out if he jumps now. He's got so much life ahead of him.

What about the others? They'd surely miss him. I think about Avery, Sybil, Vaughn, Harrison, Emma, Florence, and Emerson. All his friends will miss him. Where are they? Someone will come and stop him. Anyone. Please.

I can't do anything else but watch as he slowly loosens his grip on the rusty beams, closing his puffy eyes, his wet eyelashes making him look so at peace with himself as he leans forward. His toes leave the metal railing, forming perfect points, as if he was leaping through the air instead of falling toward the rough waters.

A scream escapes my mouth, but I know he didn't hear me. No one did.

I'm not sure what takes over my body, but I feel the coolness of the wind ripping through my hair as I realize I'm diving in after him. A loud smack breaks through the sound of the rapids as his body makes contact with the water. Another smack must have echoed seconds later as my body hits the freezing water just behind him. All the grace he once held disappears as his limbs twist and tangle with the current, the impact of the fall making him instantly fall unconscious. His head dips below the surface and I dive, pushing my arms against the current to get to him. I lose track of his tall frame for a second and can only hope I'm swimming in the right direction. Unsure if he survived a fall from that height and into those rough waters, I find myself whispering a small prayer to DD's god.

Does anyone know he's here? How will they find him? Will they know to look here? Of course, they won't. No one will think to look here. That's why it's such a great place to end it. It's somewhere no one will think to look and be able to stop you from jumping. That's what I would've thought too. As much as I long for someone to relate to and understand my situation, I don't want this life for Noah. Having to struggle to find a purpose, being frozen in time, not knowing who you are, where you came from, or where you are supposed to go, or who you're supposed to be. Being emotionally pushed around by a past you don't have any memories from, but all the same reactions to. Tiptoeing around while the rest of the world moves forward without a second thought. I wouldn't want this for anyone.

I frantically scan my eyes over the water's choppy surface, but I can't seem to spot him. After what feels like hours of watery-eyed searching, I finally spot his limp body up against a large log sticking out from between two boulders near the center of the river. Ignoring the pain in my limbs and screaming in my throat, I force myself closer to him. My purple fingers instinctly wrap around his frame, his body feeling heavier than I imagined it'd be as I try to carry his limp body toward the riverbank. I'm only able to move him two feet before we are swept with the current, my head plunging beneath the surface again. I fight to keep him afloat, knowing he needs the air to breathe unlike me. The water burns my throat, and red flashes of my own death start to resurface, of wanting to die myself.

Die worthless whore.

I can't let him die. This is Noah, one of the boys I watched grow up, playing with his friends, and learning to dance. He was so passionate and dedicate. Marvel even compared him to Pierre Dulaine. It was so blissful to dance with him at the studio.

Was I like this? Alone, with no one to protect me but oblivious to my own gifts?

I have to protect him.

Maneuvering Noah's body so that my feet are on his back and my head is moving closest toward the direction of the current, I kick his body once more with all the strength I can conjure, knowing we can't be that far from the bank now. My eyes burn against the water as I let the current wash me away from Noah's body, his feet still visible at the edge of the river.

Pain consumes me as his body disappears, and I swallow more water, the rapids seeming to get more intense. Is this it? Am I going to become a Shell now? I guess it was worth it since I saved Noah.

Suddenly, two little blue hands pop into view, reaching out to me in the water before I'm able to close my eyes and fall into the coolness completely. I reach up and clasp onto the hands, letting myself get pulled to the surface, gasping for air as I'm thrust onto the patchy gravel. A familiar scent of jasmine and roses wafts into my nose, and my eyelids fly open to see DD's small blue frame lying next to me on the gravel.

I'm different now. I not alone anymore.

"You sure are crazy, River," she laughs, flipping over onto her back, staring up at the greenish-blue sky. "But I'm glad you jumped after him. That kiddo is too young to pass on just yet," she says, smirking up at the wispy clouds.

"Okay, Travis," I laugh, flipping over so I'm looking up at the sky too. I put my hands in front of me, noticing the purple color still lingering at my fingertips.

I saved him.

"I can't believe I just did that," I say, clenching and unclenching my hands as if they'd change back to blue or alter this new reality.

"I guess I was wrong," DD sighs, scrunching her face as

she closes her eyes. "I don't' really know what is happening to you, but I've never seen it before."

"We'll just have to figure it out together then," I reply, smiling back at her before sitting up. "Where is Noah?"

"The boy is over there," she says lazily, pointing to her left, back toward the direction of the bridge, not bothering to open her eyes.

Scrapping myself off the ground, I let my bare feet push against the pointy gravel ground, ignoring the slight pinching I now feel as I race toward Noah's limp body. I stop just before him, noting his body isn't blue nor is there a bluish version of himself lingering around his waking-life body. I stare at his chest carefully, seeing slight movement as his ribcage rises at a sloth-like pace. He's alive. And I saved him.

Acknowledgments

There have been so many people that have shaped me to become the person I am, who have encouraged me to pursue and study writing. My mom, Julie Van Buskirk, has always been my emotional support through life's journey. My dad, David Van Buskirk, has always been my number one fan, giving me the momentum to study the thing I love, writing. My brothers and sister, Benjamin Carvajal, Rachel Van Buskirk, and Cisco Carvajal have been my best friends through live, sticking by me and listening to my endless dreams and ideas for stories and loving me through it all. My friends, Virginia Horn, Gloria Harmon, and Bernadette Goolsby have been my sound board and editors through this whole process and I couldn't have done it without them. It was while writing this piece that I met the love of my life, Andrew McDonald. He was the first to read the finished product and continues to give me endless support through my writing adventures. My professors, Aimee Parkison, Timothy Murphy, and Laura Minor have been such amazing mentors while writing this story. Thank you all for being such incredible people in my life, allowing me to grow and learn from you all. I wouldn't be the same person without any of you.

About the Author

Sarah Carvajal earned an MFA and her bachelors degrees in Creative Writing at Oklahoma State University and has taught English courses at Oklahoma State University. Her work highlights how societal and familiar strife effects the female mind through the lens of the fantastic. She is currently working at a local magazine in sales and marketing near the town she grew up, spending her free time with her friends and family when she isn't writing or drinking coffee. She is also a co-owner of a budding luxury clothing brand, Maiden, launching in 2026.

Made in the USA
Coppell, TX
15 September 2025

54818333R00069